The Pilgrimage:

Snow White's Dual

Co-Authors; Jane Murdock & Mark Nelson

Dedication

To our parents — the first guardians of our stories.

You gave us the gift of life, and with it, the unshakable roots of love, faith, and courage. Every step we take on this Pilgrimage, every trial faced, is possible because of the light you placed within us. You have always stood as our protectors and encouragers, shaping us into the people we are today.

This book is more than a tale; it is an offering of gratitude. Thank you for raising two strong, stubborn, kick-ass souls who dared to dream and to walk their own path. The strength of this journey belongs not only to us, but to you—for you built the foundation, you believed before we did, and you loved us into being.

May this story echo the truth we've always known: we are who we are because of you.

__Prologue__

Somewhere between the realms of the living and the damned, there lies a place where even silence forgets itself.

It is not night here, though neither is it day. Time itself seems hesitant, caught in an endless breath, unwilling to move forward lest it awaken the dead things that slumber beneath the sands. A muted sepia pall hangs over the ruins, staining all that was once regal into a jaundiced memory of decay. It is here, in the center of what was once a grand courtyard, that she lies.

Snow White.

Her body is half-covered in dust and a veil of fine sand, as if the earth itself tried to swallow her whole but forgot to finish the deed. She does not stir yet, though a tremor beneath her ribs suggests that life remains—stubborn, flickering, reluctant.

Around her, the remnants of sovereignty rot. Shattered statues of kings and queens jut out of the ground like bones picked clean. Their marble faces, where still intact, seem caught in expressions of despair or rage, mouths agape as if they had tried to scream long after their heads were cleaved from their stone shoulders.

A throne, once the seat of power, lies face-down in the dirt, its gilded back cracked down the middle. Not far from it grows a tree, or what might have once been called such—its trunk twisted and blackened, its limbs clawing at the ashen sky as if pleading for mercy that will never come.

The ground itself is a palimpsest of former grandeur and violent ruin. Shards of stained glass, dulled by grit, catch faint and sickly light, their colors muted but persistent—fragments of forgotten saints, broken angels, and devils disguised in halos.

And then she breathes.

Slow. Shallow. As though the act itself pains her. Her chest rises, but the motion is heavy, as if something enormous sits atop her heart. When her eyes flicker open, their whites are greyed with exhaustion, their pupils slow to focus on the bleak world before her.

There is no sound save the distant, untraceable murmurs—the half-sounds of memory or ghost. Yet even in the quiet, her heart pounds loud within her chest, each throb dragging a

sensation of unbearable weight. She is not simply tired; she is burdened, as though her very soul carries the debris of a thousand collapsed kingdoms.

Her fingers twitch, brushing against the sand and stone, seeking an anchor in the ruin. She does not yet rise. She only feels. The sorrow of the place. The familiarity of loss. The accusing silence of broken thrones.

She does not know yet where she is. But the ashes in her lungs remembers:

She has failed.

And failure here tastes like dust rusted by regret.

Yet the air stirs.

Not a wind, but a *presence*. Something enters the periphery of this dead place—a shift, a tremor of peace displacing despair. The weight on her heart lessens—not lifted, but stilled, like storm waters suddenly becalmed.

Before she can make sense of it, she feels him.

Warmth—not of flesh, but of spirit. An unassuming calm that settles into the bones and spreads outward like dawn's first light. The murmurs that once haunted the courtyard fall silent, as though the world itself holds its breath.

She sees him then.

He stands nearby—not above her, not before her—but simply with her. A figure pale and cloaked, familiar as a dream long forgotten. His cloak is long, worn but clean, the shade of weathered parchment. Beneath it, his garb is simple—a tunic of deep grey, trousers bound with leather at the calves, and boots dusted from many roads. His face is youthful yet weary, bearing the softness of compassion tempered by the hardness of trial. His hair is dark and loosely tied at the nape, strands escaping like shadows of a forgotten past.

His eyes are the most striking—a soft, steady brown, deep as fertile earth, with a gaze that neither condemns nor pities. They see through her, into her, and find no need to turn away.

No words pass his lips. He does not need them. His presence alone is a language she somehow understands.

He extends his hand.

Snow stares, her thoughts—wild and accusing only moments before—now silenced. It is as though every bitter voice within her mind has been dismissed by his mere presence.

Tentatively, she lifts her hand to meet his. His touch is cool, not cold—like marble beneath the sun—and when he pulls her gently upward, the ache in her body remains, but the unbearable sorrow in her heart is paused.

She stands.

They face one another, eye to eye. There is no dominance between them, no command. Yet in the marrow of her bones, she senses the truth: she has met a gatekeeper—not of stone, but of souls. And though he speaks no word, something within her knows.

The path still waits. And he is here to guide—should she choose to walk.

It stretches ahead, a narrow artery of uneven cobblestones, flanked by crumbling relics of long forgotten German design. Half-timbered houses lean precariously, their bones exposed where walls have rotted away. Gabled rooftops sag, shingles missing like teeth knocked from a dying mouth. Murals, once brilliant with scenes of saints and sinners, are now mottled with grime, their faces smeared and eyeless.

Christian walks beside her, step for step. In his right hand, he carries a shepherd's staff—gnarled, the wood stained dark with time. Carvings wind up its length: miniature reliefs of his pilgrimage—The Wicket Gate, Vanity Fair, the Valley of the Shadow of Death, the Celestial City. Each image is small but intricate, as though the staff carries a living memory of every place his feet have trodden.

Beyond the road, a blurred expanse stretches on either side—about a hundred yards before clarity is swallowed whole by distortion. It is as if the world has forgotten to finish painting itself. But the sounds within that blur are anything but forgetful.

Vulture-like birds croak and beat their heavy wings just beyond sight. The slithering drag of massive scales etches patterns into the ruins, while the scuttling of countless insect legs—too many, too sharp—clatter against unseen stone.

Yet beyond the veil of blur, there is more.

Shadowy spirits and monstrous shapes flit and surge chaotically, pressing against the boundary like moths battering glass. Their forms are erratic—some skeletal, others fleshy and bulbous, eyes glowing like coals. They scratch and claw, howling voicelessly, desperate to breach the divide.

But they do not.

Not yet.

Snow hears them. She knows they are there. But she does not flinch. She walks. Because the alternative—the stopping—is an invitation.

With every step, the realization anchors itself deeper:

She is dead.

There is no heartbeat, no hunger, no thirst. Only burden. Only the weight of unfinished reckonings.

Beside her, Christian walks in silence. His gaze remains ahead, staff steady, pace unwavering.

And so they walk the road of the dead—one step, one breathless moment at a time—into the blur, where the path is the only thing that still remembers its own shape.

***

They had been walking for some time now. How long, neither could say. In this place, time did not stretch or pass—it hovered, unmeasured, a breath never exhaled.

The path continued its winding descent through a world quietly unraveling. The gabled silhouettes of ruined Germanic houses loomed like bowed heads on either side. Beyond the hundred-yard reach of clarity, the blur thickened, and with it came the monstrous echoes—the scrape of scaled bellies, the low hiss of wings too large to be natural, and the haunting clatter of legs that skittered by the thousands.

But here on the path, it was still.

Snow's steps had steadied, though her mind wandered far. Each footfall fell in time with Christian's, as if they shared one rhythm. She had not spoken since they began, but now—at last—she did.

Her voice was soft, distant, not sorrowful but contemplative. "Does it ever truly matter, what we choose?"

Christian did not stop walking. He did not turn his head. But the quiet seemed to bend, leaning toward her as he listened.

"I mean," she continued, eyes fixed ahead, "if this... all of this... is the outcome, was there ever another road? Or do we only fool ourselves into thinking we steer anything at all?"

A long silence followed. Not of neglect, but of reverence.

Then he spoke.

"God's plan is inevitable," he said, his tone even and sure. "But inevitability is not predestination."

Snow glanced at him, waiting.

"The ending is written," he went on, "but the ink used to write it is drawn from every soul who lives. Your choices were not illusions, Snow. They were echoes. They mattered. They still do."

He gripped the staff in his hand gently. The carvings along its wood glimmered faintly, as if warmed by the truth.

"Be cautious," he added, voice deepening slightly, "not to mistake the shape of a river for the stillness of a pond. The current moves with or without you. But it is your swimming, your striving, your surrendering... that changes the current's song."

Snow was quiet. The weight in her chest did not leave, but it shifted—gathering into something not quite lighter, but clearer.

The road hummed beneath their feet—a low, muted resonance, like an old hymn trapped in stone.

Snow walked beside Christian in silence, but her mind had long since ceased its stillness. The questions had risen slowly, then all at once, like floodwater breaching a rotted gate. At last, she spoke.

"What is this path we tread, truly?"

Her voice did not waver. It rang with an echoing calm, as if spoken not only to him, but to the grey and broken heavens above.

"Are we bound for the Himmlische Jerusalem? The Eternal Light?"

She paused, scanning the air, thick with ash and fading silhouettes. "Surely not," she added. "This realm is too cold for the Lamb's embrace. Too silent for angels."

Christian said nothing. His eyes, warm and ancient, held hers for only a breath, then turned back to the road.

"And yet you walk beside me with staff in hand, carved like a prophet's ledger," she continued. "Are you one of the Seraphim? Or merely a steward of the dead?"

A gust stirred dust across their boots. Beyond the hundred-yard veil, something shrieked and scrambled, clawing at the boundary.

"Perhaps," she said more softly now, "this is the Abgrund—the Abyss. The Kingdom of the Lost. Am I being judged in secret? Measured and unwound by your silence?"

Her hand trembled briefly at her side. Still, she walked.

"Or is this the Immerkreis? The old folk whispered of it—the circle that devours itself, births itself, lives again. Have I failed in one life, only to begin another, cursed to forget until I fail anew?"

She looked up toward the pale, ailing sky.

"Did I misplace my soul upon the wrong altar? Was the Lamb I followed only a silhouette in the dark?"

Still, Christian did not answer.

But there was a glimmer at the edge of his eye—something between mirth and mercy.

Snow's breath caught in her throat. Her voice lowered to a whisper.

"Was I ever meant to know the truth at all? Or am I only meant to walk?

Christian's gaze stayed ahead, but at last, his voice came—low, patient, tinged with something that might have been the gentlest humor.

"You ask as one who still believes answers will come before the end."

Snow blinked, startled by his tone more than his words. She scoffed quietly, not unkindly. "An angel fond of riddles."

He smiled at that—only faintly, but it was there.

Then the air shifted. The road beneath them trembled—not violently, but like a deep breath held just too long. A strange light rippled through the blur on the horizon, not golden, but ancient—like the glow of firelight behind stone.

Snow slowed her pace. She felt it before she could name it. The presence of something vast. A threshold.

"You feel it," Christian said, now speaking fully, solemnly. "It draws near."

Snow looked at him, her brow furrowed. "A gate?"

"A crossing," he answered. "A reckoning. You are about to enter the Duat."

Her lips parted, a whisper escaping. She had heard the word before—in stories, in warnings, in scripture buried beneath scripture.

"There is no turning back," Christian said. "This is your pilgrimage. The path is no longer suggestion, but command."

She swallowed. "And if I fail again?"

He looked at her, not as a judge, but as one who has walked hard roads beside many.

"Then you fail honestly. And the Duat does not forget honesty."

He turned forward once more. "The only road to the Celestial City… is through."

They walked in silence then, the veil thinning ahead like breath on glass.

And then—he stopped.

Snow did as well, instinct drawing her to face him. Christian turned toward her fully for the first time, his gaze steady, his presence no longer merely companion but threshold.

The stillness deepened.

When he spoke, it was like a prayer carved in stone:

"Remember this upon your pilgrimage—though you may feel abandoned, though shadows may convince you that the heavens have turned their face, you are never alone."

His voice did not waver, though it carried the weight of centuries.

"You never have been. And if you endure—if you complete the road laid before you—the path shall lead you unto eternal peace."

He paused.

"Good luck, Snow White."

She turned.

And there it stood: a towering door of darkened wood, arched and ancient—an exact replica of her own throne room's door, down to the etched lilies and golden hinges. But it was larger here. Grand and terrible. Waiting.

Snow stepped toward it. She did not look back.

Her hand pressed against the wood. It groaned open.

She walked through and entered the Duat.

Trial 1: Temptations Crown

"Be sober-minded; be watchful.

Your adversary the devil prowls around like a roaring lion,

seeking someone to devour."

1 Peter 5:8

Snow stepped through the door, and at once the silence fell upon her like a shroud. The throne room stretched before her—unchanged, yet unreal, as though carved from memory and shadow. Stone walls breathed with a dim light, their familiar patterns wavering as though reflected in dark waters. Her throne loomed at the far end, tall and unyielding, a crown of iron and sorrow resting invisible above it.

A heat stirred in her chest. First faint, then consuming—rage, sharp and venomous, blooming like a black rose. It coiled around her heart, smothering reason, veiling the truth of where she stood. Her breath grew ragged, and her vision blurred with crimson edges, until all she saw was betrayal: the faces that had smiled, the voices that had whispered, the world that had cheered her downfall.

Her hands trembled—not from weakness, but from the gnawing ache of sovereignty stolen. *Why had she ever been chosen to reign, if only to be undone by treachery?* The thought seared her mind, blinding her to the mystical air of trial that now enfolded her.

And then—movement.

From behind her throne, a ripple of shadow stirred. The air thickened, heavy as desert wind before a storm. A form lingered at the edge of sight, not yet revealed, but vast, deliberate. She felt its eyes upon her, though it made no sound.

Snow's jaw tightened. She took a step closer, fists clenched at her sides, her voice low and bitter:

"Show yourself, usurper… thief of crowns."

The veil of rage thickened around her, but so too did the shadows begin to answer.

A silence stretched, long enough that Snow's words seemed to bleed into the stone itself. Then, it came—low at first, then swelling into the vastness of the chamber: a laugh. Mocking, guttural, and steeped in ancient scorn.

The sound curled along the vaulted ceiling like smoke from a battlefield pyre. It was no mortal mirth but the hardened rasp of one who had tasted centuries of war, of blood spilt and kingdoms broken. It bore the weight of deserts and the cruelty of storms, the voice of a sovereign not made by hand but forged by strife.

"*Usurper?*" the voice rumbled, each syllable rolling like thunder through cracked earth. "Child-queen, how naïve you remain. Did you truly believe your crown was ever your own to claim? You were placed upon that seat by a will far greater than your feeble hands could grasp. Even your birthright was not your doing, but the decree of powers far above you."

The laugh returned, harsher now—like iron striking iron.

"You speak of thrones and thefts as though sovereignty were ever yours to command. *I have walked through empires that crumbled into dust, reigned where gods themselves quailed, and waged wars long before your bloodline ever dreamed of glory.*"

The shadows thickened behind the throne, curling forward like talons stretching to touch her rage. She could not yet see the form, but his presence filled the chamber, vast and unyielding.

"Snow White," the voice growled, low and deliberate, "you are but a sovereign on borrowed breath. And I—I am the one wronged, the one denied. Do not call me usurper, for *I am the measure of kings.*"

Snow's breath caught. His words had struck deeper than she wished to admit. Fear coiled beneath her rage, cold and sharp, as if it was cracking deep in her bones—there was truth in his scorn. Her arrogance, her defiance, all crumbled beneath the thunder of his voice. Yet still, her blood burned. For he meant to belittle her, to strip her pride bare before the throne that had once been hers.

A hush pressed down on the chamber, as though the air itself awaited his will. Then, with a growl that trembled through the stone, he declared:

"I am the measure of kings."

The shadows obeyed.

From behind the throne, the figure stepped forth. Not a whisper, not a hesitation—he moved with the unyielding certainty of one who had never bowed. His armor was pure gold, though dulled and scarred by countless battles, its plates etched not with jewels but with wounds of war. Each mark spoke of conquests in deserts where the sun itself shrieked in fury, where the sands drank the blood of those foolish enough to stand against him. The metal seemed to carry the echo of ancient screams, as though it had been forged not from earth, but from the marrow of fallen gods.

His form was unmistakable: the deity Set, features carved by the cruelty of storms and the relentlessness of war. He bore the jackal's crown upon his helm, a visage of dread and authority that demanded silence. His eyes burned—not with fire, but with a feral light that devoured weakness wherever it lingered. To look upon him was to be undone. He was not merely a king; he was the father of kings, a sovereign forged from chaos itself.

He stepped with deliberate weight, each movement a declaration of dominion, until he reached her throne. Without pause, without acknowledgment of her presence, he turned and sat—settling upon the seat as though it had always belonged to him.

The silence thickened. Authority radiated from him, unfiltered, absolute. The chamber itself seemed to bow.

From the corner of her vision, Snow felt movement: the Sha. The beast did not snarl, did not strike. It only *was*—a looming shadow at her side, pressing close, its presence felt more in her bones than on her skin. Slowly, inexorably, it heeled her forward, drawing her toward the figure upon her throne.

Set waited, saying nothing. His silence was more terrible than his words, for it commanded one truth: in his presence, *she was not sovereign.*

He leaned back upon her throne, his golden armor groaning faintly with the weight of forgotten wars. His gaze fixed on her—unyielding, dissecting, a predator's patience writ in divine form. Slowly, his eyes traveled the length of her, not with desire, but with judgment, as though measuring a blade dulled by misuse.

The silence pressed tighter. Every breath Snow took seemed to echo too loudly, every heartbeat like a drum announcing her weakness. Her rage, which moments before had seemed a roaring fire, now felt fragile beneath that stare—like embers suffocating under ash.

And yet, in that crucible of silence, the embers stirred. The longer he gazed, the more her blood seethed. Her jaw locked. Her fists clenched. Rage rose to shield her against the terror that threatened to swallow her whole.

Only then did he move.

His head tilted, eyes narrowing as though reading the storm within her. When he finally spoke, his voice was no longer mocking laughter, but the gravel-born rumble of stone dragged across stone—ancient, scarred, unrelenting.

"Your rage betrays you," he said, the words striking like hammers. "Tell me, Snow White—what did all your strivings bring? What did your sleepless nights, your sacrifices, your blood and sweat purchase for you?"

He leaned forward, the gold of his armor catching the dim light like fire licked by shadow.

"Another sits upon your throne."

The words fell heavy, undeniable, shattering the veil of pride she tried to hold.

Set's stare did not waver. His silence after was more cruel than his voice, for it demanded her answer—not with words, but with the very fracture of her spirit.

Snow's lips parted, her voice trembling at first, then sharpening as the fire within her pushed against the weight of his stare.

"They never saw," she hissed, fists tightening at her sides. "Not once did they look upon me and understand what I bore for them. Every choice I made, every sacrifice—twisted into blame, spat back in my face. I kept the wolves from the gates, I fed the starving, I carved order from chaos... and still, they whispered treason. Still, they called me tyrant."

Her breath quickened, rage spilling like venom. "They never cared for the blood I spilled to guard them. They rejoiced at my downfall, as if my ruin were their salvation. Even my own—" her voice cracked, though she forced it steady, "my own kingdom turned against me. Always *us* against *them*. Never gratitude, never loyalty… only knives."

The words echoed bitterly through the chamber, clinging to the stone like smoke. Her eyes burned with unshed fury, her body trembling not with weakness but with the weight of betrayal too long buried.

Set did not interrupt. His silence stretched wide, deliberate. And yet Snow felt him there, behind the stillness—guiding, urging, pulling her words into place as though each syllable were already written.

At last, he stirred. A slow incline of his head, the faint curl of something that might have been approval—or triumph. His voice rumbled forth, low and deliberate, worn by centuries of conquest.

"Yes," he growled. "They betrayed you. They scorned the hand that bled for them. And what is the fruit of their contempt?"

The shadows thickened around the throne, curling like a veil ready to fall. His words came heavy, purposeful, laden with promise.

"You will see, Snow White. You will see what your labors bought you… and what was squandered."

Set's gaze lingered, unblinking, as her words faded into the heavy silence. When he spoke again, it was not with mockery but with a terrible weight, as though the stones themselves carried his voice.

"You are right," he said, his tone a growl deep as thunder rolling across a desert sky. "You were betrayed. Wronged beyond measure. Those you guarded spat upon your crown. They feasted upon your labor and rejoiced at your ruin. Yes, Snow White… you were wronged."

The words hung, tempting her heart to rest in them. But then his voice shifted—harder, jagged, cutting through her pride like a blade.

"But do not mistake yourself for some innocent lamb led to slaughter. You are no blameless victim. You were sovereign—ruthless, merciless, a queen whose hands were not clean but crimson. Your reign was no holy martyrdom. It was blood and iron. And it failed."

15

Snow flinched, though she did not look away. Rage flickered in her eyes, but beneath it, shame stirred like a serpent uncoiling.

Set leaned forward, gold armor catching dim light in broken gleams, his presence filling every breath of the chamber.

"You wish to remember yourself as betrayed," he said, voice low and merciless. "But I will show you the truth. A ruler undone not only by others' treachery, but by her own missteps—her own pride, her own blindness, her own failings."

His jackal-helmed visage tilted, eyes burning with cruel authority. A slow, deliberate smile crept across his scarred lips.

"Come then, Snow White," he growled, savoring the words. "Let us take a look at some of your greatest failures."

***

The First Failure: Squandered Grace

The shadows quivered like veils, and the throne room dissolved. Stone gave way to light, music, and the roar of celebration. Snow blinked, her breath catching, for she stood once more in her wedding hall.

Golden banners swept down from vaulted rafters, roses bloomed in every corner, and the sound of harps filled the air. A sea of faces looked upon her—nobles and peasants alike—cheering, weeping, calling her blessed. At her side stood her prince, her charming, flawless, fairy-tale groom, a smile sculpted for ballads. Snow, clothed in white so pure it nearly blinded the eye, seemed to embody grace itself.

Set's voice slithered through the music, harsh as stone grinding in desert wind. "Ah yes… your grand day. A spectacle worthy of song. Luxury unmatched, a fairy tale fulfilled. Here, the child-queen ascended not only a throne, but the hearts of her people."

His tone darkened, mocking. "Or so they thought."

The laughter and music fractured. The hall seemed to shudder, and from its far edge, a figure was dragged forward.

Snow watched, her younger self radiant upon the dais, gaze sharp with satisfaction. Servants carried forth a cruel gift: a pair of iron shoes, glowing red from the fire, smoke hissing as they touched the air.

Set's voice dripped with scorn, filling every corner of the vision. "And here—your mercy was tested. Grace placed in your hands, Snow White. The chance to show the world that innocence had not withered in your heart. That sovereignty could rise above vengeance."

The Queen shrieked as the shoes were brought forth, her body trembling in terror. She begged, stumbling to her knees, her voice cracking against the cheers of the hall. The guests laughed, clapping, chanting for her punishment.

Snow's younger self rose, her wedding gown shimmering like fresh-fallen snow. She looked down upon the broken woman, lips curling—not with mercy, but with judgment. With a wave of her hand, the order was given.

The shoes were strapped to the Queen's feet.

A scream ripped through the hall, piercing, inhuman. The woman writhed, forced upright, forced to dance as the heat devoured flesh and bone. Her body convulsed, jerking to the rhythm

of her own death. The smell of burning flesh mingled with roses and wine, and the people roared their approval.

Snow's face—her own face—watched coldly, no pity in her eyes, only vindication.

Set's voice thundered above the horror, a roar that drowned the music, the screams, the cheers. "And this, Snow White, was the moment you ceased to be *the fairest of them all.*"

The Queen collapsed, smoking, her body twisted in agony, eyes wide even in death. The hall fell silent, and the vision froze.

Set's words cut like a blade: "Grace squandered. Innocence undone. A sovereign who chose cruelty when she might have chosen mercy. This was your first failure."

***

The Second Failure: Dominion Abused

The wedding hall dissolved in fire and smoke. Music and roses bled away into ash, until only silence remained. Snow's chest heaved, but the vision did not grant her breath. Shadows surged, and when they cleared, she stood upon a balcony of stone, looking out over her kingdom at war.

Below her, banners whipped in a bitter wind. The clash of steel rang from distant hills, mingling with the cries of the wounded. The dwarven village—her oldest ally, the keepers of the mines—stood vulnerable, its cottages clustered like fragile bones. Beyond it, the gemstone mine glittered faintly, as though the earth itself had bled jewels for her throne.

Set's voice coiled behind her, thunder without mercy. "Your reign was not only cruelty, Snow White. It was calculation. Dominion twisted into tyranny, all hidden behind words of necessity."

Snow's younger self stood before a gathered council, clad in armor, a crown upon her brow. Her eyes burned not with innocence, but with cold resolve.

"They come for our treasures," she declared, her voice steady, commanding. "If we lose the mines, we lose the means to rebuild, to rearm, to survive. The village can be evacuated—stone and timber can be restored. But gemstones? They are irreplaceable. We must protect the kingdom's wealth, or there will be no kingdom left."

Murmurs rose among the advisors, uncertainty flickering. But none dared oppose her word. Orders were given. The soldiers turned their march, shields and steel flowing away from the village, tightening instead around the mine.

The night came swiftly.

From the hills, torches flared like a rising tide. Enemy banners unfurled against the sky, and with a cry that split the darkness, they descended upon the undefended village.

Snow gasped as the memory unspooled—cottages engulfed in flame, dwarves screaming as their homes collapsed, mothers clutching children as fire devoured all they had built. The air was thick with smoke, with the stench of ruin.

She reached out instinctively, but the vision offered no reprieve. The dwarves, her allies, her friends, were left with nothing but ash and charred earth. Their trust was broken, their loyalty severed by betrayal that wore the mask of strategy.

Set's laughter was low, cruel, echoing through the inferno. "Dominion abused. You chose treasure over lives. You cloaked tyranny as wisdom, and in so doing, you turned allies into exiles, friends into ashes."

The fire reflected in his golden armor as he stepped closer through the vision, his eyes burning with judgment.

"You did not protect your kingdom, Snow White. You bartered its soul for glittering stones."

The village smoldered into silence. The vision froze upon the ruin, the dwarves kneeling amid the wreckage of their homes, their eyes full of betrayal.

Snow staggered as the vision of fire faded, the smoke still clinging to her breath. Her voice broke through the silence, ragged and trembling, but fierce with desperation.

"I tried to help them," she said, her eyes burning. "I made the only choice I could! What kingdom could stand without its wealth? Without strength to rebuild, we would have fallen altogether. I—" Her voice cracked, but she forced it on, bitter and breathless. "I believed it was for their good. I believed it was the only way to save them!"

Her fists trembled at her sides, her words spilling like a plea to the stone itself. "I never meant for their ruin. I thought—", Set scoffed at the words, "if I secured the mine, the kingdom could rise again. That sacrifice was temporary. That it would save countless lives in the end."

Set did not move. His eyes burned through her words, unblinking, patient as a predator. He let her spill every defense, every trembling justification, as if he savored the futility in each syllable.

When she fell silent, he leaned forward, voice a guttural growl steeped in centuries of war.

"You *believed.*" The word dripped with scorn, echoing through the chamber like a curse. "You clothed selfish dominion in the garb of necessity. You call betrayal salvation, and ruin strategy. But Snow White—your belief did not heal them. It did not save them."

He rose, towering in his scarred gold, and the chamber trembled at his step. His hand lifted, as though to silence her very breath.

"Enough. Do not speak of what you *meant*. History does not remember intentions. It remembers only what you do."

His voice deepened, a rumble that shook her bones.
"You say you tried to help?"

The shadows surged, pulling at the air, dragging her downward as though the stone itself betrayed her. The throne room dissolved again, smoke and fire sucked away into a darker memory still.

"Then let us look," Set snarled, "at what became of your helping hand."

***

The Third Failure: Completion Corrupted

The fire faded, ashes swept away like sand in a storm. Snow steadied herself, only to find the village before her once more—yet it was not ruin she beheld, but splendor.

The cottages gleamed, their walls carved with delicate artistry, their beams polished, their windows bright with colored glass. Markets bustled, fountains glittered, laughter echoed from the streets. To any passerby, it looked as though tragedy had been erased, replaced by beauty a thousand times more radiant than before.

Set's voice rumbled low, like distant thunder rolling over dunes. "Behold... your mercy. Your helping hand. Your promise fulfilled."

Snow's younger self walked through the streets, her gown trailing behind her, as master craftsmen bowed low, eager to please their queen. Their tools flashed, their hammers rang, and in every corner rose new works of art, perfect and gleaming.

But the air was wrong. The laughter hollow. The beauty brittle.

Within the rebuilt cottages, the dwarves sat in silence. Their hands rested on tables that bore no marks of their fathers. Their walls held paintings not passed from mother to child, but brushed by foreign hands. Their hearths glowed, but the warmth was cold.

Generations of history, of love and memory, had been swept aside like rubble. Priceless relics lost to the fire were replaced by shallow replicas, their beauty empty, their meaning dead.

And there—by one doorway—Happy stood. His once-joyful face heavy, his eyes sunk in sorrow. He lingered in the crowd, unmoving. For the briefest heartbeat, his gaze seemed to shift—not to the radiant queen in the memory, but beyond, to the Snow who stood in the Duat.

Snow froze. Did he see her? Did he know?

But the moment was gone. He looked away, folding back into the illusion, swallowed by the sorrow of his people.

Set's voice grew sharper, crueler. "You called this restoration. But it was desecration. You gave them new walls and shining windows, but you buried their fathers' hearthstones. You erased their history, their blood, their very souls... and called it salvation."

The streets fell silent. The dwarves' hollow stares pierced deeper than flames had. Snow's younger self walked proudly among them, blind to their grief, her head lifted as though she had done them honor.

Set's words thundered over the scene, final and merciless.

"This was *Completion Corrupted.* You did not restore. You replaced. And in your haste to ease your guilt, you mocked the very ashes of their loss."

The jeweled village shimmered, but no warmth flowed from it. Snow felt the silence of its people crushing down like a tomb. Then Set's voice rolled through the stillness, deeper, harsher than before—like a storm breaking stone.

"Look well, Snow White. This was not strength. This was not sovereignty. This was weakness draped in golden cloth."

He rose from the throne within the vision, his shadow towering over the false beauty she had wrought. His voice clawed through her chest, every word a wound.

"You were fragile. Fragile in your haste, fragile in your pride. You built walls too quickly to cover ruins you dared not look upon. And in your fear, you dressed it as mercy."

He stepped closer to her, golden armor groaning with the weight of centuries. His eyes burned with judgment.

"But above all else—" his voice thundered, the chamber shaking with the words— "your greatest crime was this: you trusted those who should never have been trusted. You gave your heart, your counsel, your throne to flatterers, liars, and parasites. And they fed on your fragility, they whispered what you wished to hear, and you obeyed. Your kingdom paid for it in blood and silence."

The vision trembled—faces of advisors flickered in the crowd, shadows of courtiers and nobles who bowed low with honeyed words, only to betray when the hour darkened. Their smiles bled into sneers, their hands filled with coin, their loyalty false.

Set's laughter broke like iron striking iron. "Not betrayed once, not betrayed twice, but *continually*—and still you opened your hand to them. A queen so desperate for faith, she offered it to jackals."

He leaned low, his breath like scorched sand, his voice a growl that rattled in her bones. "You thought yourself wise. Yet every brick you laid, every crown you wore, was mortared with *trust in the faithless*. That, Snow White, was your undoing."

The village faded, its false beauty bleeding back into shadow. Only his eyes remained, molten and merciless.

***

The Fourth Failure: Divided Loyalty

The jeweled village withered, its splendor collapsing into ash. When the smoke cleared, Snow stood not in fields or halls, but within the echo of her own cathedral—tall arches, stained glass burning with color, and banners that bore not her crest, but the sigil of her husband's church.

The air was heavy, thick with incense and judgment. Priests in black robes filled the aisles, their voices chanting like a tide of chains. And at the altar, her younger self knelt beside her prince, hands clasped in public devotion, while her crown glimmered beneath the shadow of a foreign faith.

Set's voice roared through the vaulted chamber.

"Here lies your greatest undoing—*Divided Loyalty.* You opened your gates, your altars, your throne to another's dominion. You sought to serve two masters: your kingdom, and your husband's faith. And in so doing, you served neither."

The scene shifted. Outside the cathedral, her people filled the square. Their voices once sang with freedom, with the many tongues of prayer that had bound them together. But now—silence. Soldiers patrolled the streets, banners of the Church unfurled from every window. Families who refused to bow were cast out, their homes seized, their voices drowned in edicts and decrees.

Snow's younger self raised her hand as though to speak for her kingdom, to shield them. But the priests stood higher, their shadows longer, their whispers sharper than her command.

Set's laughter shook the glass, the colors trembling like blood in light.

"You tried to stand for both. For your people, and for a husband's zeal. You tried to hold two crowns, two causes, two thrones. But a divided heart cannot rule. In seeking to serve all, you betrayed all."

The vision darkened. Behind the cathedral's veil, figures gathered in secret chambers—men of robes and rings, officials of the Church. Their whispers curled like daggers. "The Queen is not fulfilling her God-given role as protector of the faith. Under her reign, the land suffers and the common folk bear the burden. The queen has lost the mandate of heaven, and therefore her rule is no longer legitimate."

Snow gasped as the memory bled to its final cut: her own reflection, her crown torn from her brow, her throne stripped, her sovereignty swallowed by the very faith she had welcomed.

Set's voice thundered, final and merciless.

"And so they ended you. Not with armies, not with blades—but with whispers, with holy writ, with chains of faith you yourself invited. *Divided loyalty was your ruin.*"

***

The cathedral dissolved into shadow, its chants dying into silence. For a moment, Snow thought she was still within its walls, but when she blinked, the throne room surrounded her once more.

A sharp sound cut the stillness—*Caw!*

Her head snapped toward it. The Raven stood upon the cold stone floor, black wings spread wide, eyes burning like coals. Its cry seemed to split the veil of memory, rattling the haze that clung to her thoughts.

And then she saw him.

At the base of the throne, half-hidden in shadow, lay Sleepy. His small form rested against the steps, eyes closed, breath slow and steady as though in slumber. Snow's heart stilled. *Had he always been here?* She had not noticed him when the memories began, nor as Set tore her failures open one by one. Yet here he was, lying as if he belonged to the chamber.

Snow's brow furrowed. Something in her chest twisted—the Raven's cry still echoed inside her bones, pulling her to clarity. The memories... they felt wrong. *Too neat. Too cruelly framed.* For the first time, she wondered if she had been walking in another's script rather than her own.

The thought flickered like a candle against stormwind—only for an instant—before Set's shadow surged forward.

His golden armor groaned as he rose from her throne, fury etched into every line of his war-scarred face. His voice, once steady and scornful, broke into a roar that shook the very walls.

"You dare look away? You dare question what you have seen?"

The words thundered, untempered, jagged. His composure cracked, and for the first time, Snow felt not the cold authority of a god—but the raw, consuming rage of one betrayed. His eyes blazed, and his voice tore like a storm over desert sands.

"You were weak! Fragile! Faithless!" His hands clenched, trembling with wrath. "You ruined kingdom and crown alike, and still you *dare* look upon me with doubt?"

The chamber trembled with his fury, and the Raven beat its wings against the air, refusing to bow, its coal-bright eyes locked upon him.

Snow staggered back, the haze lifting further in the face of his outburst. Something in his rage betrayed him—control slipping, truth leaking through fury.

Set descended from the throne, each step a quake upon the stones. His shadow swallowed her as he closed the distance, until he loomed before her—armor scarred, jaw clenched, every muscle quivering with restrained violence.

He bent low, so close she could feel the searing heat of his breath, the vibration of fury coiled within his chest. His words no longer echoed across the hall—they tore straight into her face, venom meant only for her.

"You ungrateful wretch." The growl trembled through his teeth. "You call yourself sovereign, yet you tremble like a child at her first wound."

His eyes burned into hers, unblinking, stripping her bare.

"You squandered mercy. You betrayed allies. You desecrated history. You shackled your people beneath another man's faith. And now—you dare to stand before me as though you are *wronged?*"

Each word struck like a lash. Snow's throat tightened, but no sound came.

Set's hand lifted, not to strike, but to hover just shy of her cheek, trembling with wrath. The air blistered with his heat. His voice dropped to a guttural whisper, more cruel than his roar.

"Everything you touched turned to ash. And still—you will not admit it."

His teeth bared, lips curling into something between a snarl and a smile.

"You are not queen. You are failure incarnate. You are not the fairest, not the purest, not the chosen. You are a hollow crown, draped upon a trembling girl who never deserved the throne she sat upon."

Snow's breath hitched. She could not move. His presence devoured her, every syllable burrowing into her soul like iron spikes.

Set leaned closer still, his scarred armor pressing, his breath like fire. "You were nothing then... and you are nothing now."

The words hung, poisonous, sinking deep into silence.

Set's words still burned in her chest when his tone shifted. The fury did not vanish, but curled inward, softening into something more venomous still. His voice dropped, almost tender, the whisper of a serpent coiled near the heart.

"But... I can change that."

Snow's eyes flickered, a shiver crawling her spine.

"I can fix what you shattered," he murmured, leaning so close his breath scorched her cheek. "I can undo the ruin. I can give back what was stolen from you."

He drew back only a fraction, golden armor groaning, eyes never leaving hers.

"Your parents restored to life, reigning in peace. *You,* beloved and sovereign, no longer mocked or betrayed. And your children—your bloodline—throne-bound in glory. Three generations of prosperity: your parents, yourself, and your children. Happiness unbroken, peace unchallenged."

The chamber rippled. The shadows stirred, and the Sha padded forward from the edges of the room. The beast's body quivered, its form melting, reshaping. Fur twisted into flesh, muzzle contorting, eyes shifting from predator to man. And before her, where the monstrous hound had stood, rose a figure of perfection—*Prince Charming.*

Golden hair gleamed, his jaw sculpted, his smile steady, his armor flawless. He moved with a devotion that seemed unbreakable, his eyes locked to hers in radiant loyalty. He bowed low before her, and when he rose, his hand extended—not in hunger, but in fealty.

Set's voice thundered, steady now, poisoned with promise.

"And he will be yours. No longer a phantom groom, no longer a fairy-tale farce. He will be your fearless king, your loyal sovereign at your side. Every choice you make, he will stand with you. Every trial, he will strengthen you. You will never be alone, never betrayed, never abandoned again."

The vision swelled—her throne filled with light, her parents smiling beside her, her children laughing in halls of peace, her husband's hand clasped firmly in hers. The world restored, perfected.

Set's hand lifted, palm outstretched, heavy with golden authority. His eyes locked on hers, unyielding.

"All of this can be yours, Snow White. All you need do… is take my hand."

Snow's lips parted, her voice unsteady, trembling as if pulled by unseen strings.

"What… what would I have to do?" she whispered, her eyes still locked on the shining vision of her parents, her throne, her children. "What price is hidden in this gift? What downfall follows such a promise?"

Set's smile curved slow and predatory, scarred lips stretched across teeth that gleamed like a wolf's beneath golden armor. He leaned close, his breath hot against her ear, every movement sending a pulse of fire through her veins, adrenaline rushing as though her very blood bent to his will.

"There is no downfall, Snow White," he purred, voice rich, honeyed with false sweetness. "Only devotion. Only truth. You need but serve me—*the King of Kings*. Forever devoted. Forever mine. Every choice you make will be sanctified in my will, every breath you take secured in my shadow. Through me, your crown will never be stolen again."

Snow's body quivered, confusion burning in her chest. The words filled her with heat, with trembling power, and yet—something writhed in her soul, something wrong. His nearness was suffocating, intoxicating, a fire that promised both life and ruin.

Her lips parted to speak, to surrender or to question again—when it came.

Caw!

The Raven's cry shattered the chamber like glass. Its echo boomed along the stone, filling every corner, drowning Set's velvet words in a storm of black wings.

The throne room froze. Silence devoured the promise, the vision, the lie.

Snow turned—slowly, as though in a dream—her gaze pulled from Set's burning eyes, from the outstretched hand of her false groom. She saw only the Raven, standing sentinel, its feathers shimmering with otherworldly fire.

And there—beside the throne once more—lay Sleepy. Still, silent, yet undeniably present, as though he had always been waiting.

Snow's feet moved without thought, her body trembling yet sure. She stepped away from Set, away from the golden throne, away from the illusions of restored glory. Her movements were calm, entranced, as if the god behind her no longer existed. She walked toward Sleepy, each step falling in rhythm with the Raven's call, the haze of temptation thinning with every breath.

Behind her, Set's hand still lingered in the air—open, waiting—but she did not turn back.

Snow knelt, her knees trembling as she lowered herself beside Sleepy's small form. His chest rose and fell with the rhythm of endless slumber, his face calm, untouched by shadow or flame. She leaned closer, hesitant, her hand hovering as though even this act might break the fragile stillness of the chamber.

Above her, the Raven spread its wings wide, a storm of black feathers glimmering with starlight. Its eyes burned, urging her onward, its silent command clearer than words.

Snow swallowed hard, breath quickening. She looked back down, her hand trembling as it reached for Sleepy's shoulder. She only meant to move him, to shift him from his place by the throne.

But the moment her fingers brushed his sleeve—

—*the world split open.*

The veil of rage, of resentment, of betrayal, shattered like glass. Shadows dissolved, illusions broke apart, and light poured in like water flooding a cracked tomb.

The wedding—no longer cruelty, but joy. Her people had not roared for vengeance, but for celebration, their hearts united in her happiness.

The dwarves—not abandoned, but defended. She saw herself standing at the gates with them, fighting shoulder to shoulder as the enemy broke upon their courage.

The village—not desecrated, but restored with love. Families rebuilt their homes with their own hands, songs rising from the ruins, their history honored, not erased.

Her kingdom—not shackled beneath one faith, but strengthened by her stand for freedom. She saw herself defying even her husband's zeal, shielding her people from tyranny until her last breath.

Snow gasped, tears spilling unbidden. The memories she had borne twisted in cruelty were not truth but poison. Her people had not despised her. They had *stood with her*. Through failure, through fire, through betrayal, they had loved her still.

Her chest heaved as the final truth washed over her: Every mistake had been met not with abandonment, but with loyalty. Every wound had carved wisdom. Every burden had made her courageous. She had been flawed—but never forsaken.

Snow's hand lingered on Sleepy's shoulder, her body bowed in silence. Above, the Raven let out a single echoing caw that rolled through the chamber like a bell of judgment, silencing even the shadows.

Snow rose slowly from Sleepy's side, her hand falling gently back to her side. The haze was gone, her vision clear, her heart steady. Her breath no longer came in ragged gasps, but in calm, measured strength.

She turned to face him.

Set still loomed in golden armor, his false groom gleaming at his side, his hand outstretched in cruel invitation. Yet his presence no longer shook her. The fire of his breath, the weight of his fury, the shimmer of his promise — all had lost their hold.

Snow's lips curved, not in scorn, but in calm resolve. Her voice rang soft, but each word struck with unshakable weight.

"Thank you… for your offer."

The chamber fell still. Even the shadows seemed to recoil at her words.

"It was tempting," she admitted, her eyes never leaving his. "You almost convinced me. Almost. You nearly wrapped me in your lies, nearly bound me in your chains. For a moment, I thought your fire might be light."

She stepped forward, and though Set's shadow pressed, she did not falter.

"But I remember," she continued, her voice lifting, steady as the toll of a bell, "the presence of the true King of Kings. His strength does not poison. His voice does not choke. His shadow does not consume. In Him, there is no haze, no rage, no hollow promise."

Her eyes burned with clarity, her chin lifted in sovereign defiance.

"I will only ever rule beneath His crown. And you—" she let the word fall like iron, "you are not He."

The Raven cawed once more, wings beating like thunder through the silence, sealing her words in the chamber.

Snow's voice did not waver as she stood before Set.

"I will not deny what I was," she said, her words steady, her gaze clear. "Yes—I was naïve. Yes—I was weak. At times, fragile. I stumbled as a queen, as a ruler of men. I bore burdens that broke me, and I faltered in judgment. Those failures are mine to own."

Her shoulders squared, her breath steady. Her eyes shone with something unbroken. "But they are not all that I was. I was loved. I was courageous. I stood when storms would have swallowed us whole. My people did not abandon me—they fought beside me. Even in my weakness, I was never alone."

She lifted her chin, her voice rising like a hymn through stone halls. "I was flawed, yes… but I was sovereign. And I was theirs."

The words rang out, not as a defense, but as truth. And as they settled, Snow felt it— sudden, unbidden, yet familiar. A weight pressing gently upon her head. Cold, metallic, heavy with memory.

Her crown.

Her hand rose instinctively, fingers brushing the circlet she knew too well—the symbol of rule, the burden and the blessing she had carried all her days. For the first time, it did not crush her. It did not poison her veins or sear her brow. She remembered it as it was meant to be—both weight and honor.

Snow stepped forward, slow and deliberate. The chamber was silent, the Raven watching from above, Set's fury seething unspoken in the dark.

Her steps echoed as she ascended the dais. Reaching the throne, she lifted the crown from her brow. She stared at it a moment, the metal gleaming with quiet reverence, and then—calmly, deliberately—she placed it upon the throne.

Not torn from her. Not stolen. Not stripped. *Given.*

Turning, she walked away. Her gown whispered across the stones as her pace did not falter, not once. And as she descended, the wall behind the throne groaned, parting. A new door yawned open, bathed in dim, beckoning light.

Snow did not look back. She stepped through the door, her heart lighter, her spirit freed. Just as she was to cross the threshold completely, she heard a final remark from Set,

"Well done, Snow White."

Trial 2: Moonlit Allemande

"Thou hast turned for me my mourning into dancing: thou hast put

off my sackcloth, and girded me with gladness."

Psalm 30:11

She stepped through the ancient door, its hinges groaning like something long entombed, and the world before her opened vast and terrible in beauty.

The heavens burned above with a brilliance she had never known. It was night, yet brighter than day; the firmament stretched wide, crowded with stars so near they seemed ready to fall upon her. Colors drifted between them, slow rivers of light that bled and folded, like the breath of eternity unveiled. The moon hung in its fullness, pale and perfect, yet it did not command the sky. Its radiance did not obscure, but deepened the splendour about it. Snow's heart ached within her breast, as though her soul had stumbled into a chamber older than time, where even silence had weight.

Her gaze lowered, and in the distance lay a lagoon. Its waters gleamed dark and still, yet every star and color above was mirrored in its surface, so that heaven seemed doubled: one stretched infinite above her, the other set for her feet. Around its edges sprawled ruins—courtyards long broken, pillars toppled, stones cracked and veiled in ivy. Shattered though they were, the stones whispered of majesty, a kingdom that had once ruled and would not be forgotten.

From above, a black shape swept across the sky. The raven descended without sound, wings wide, and came to rest upon a broken marble column. At its feet lay something bound in faded cloth, and from that bundle a corner of parchment jutted out, pale in the moonlight, trembling faintly as if alive.

Snow drew near and knelt. With hands that trembled she unwrapped the cloth, and a strip of parchment came free, its edges frayed, its words traced as though by fire. She read in silence, her lips barely moving:

Beneath the parchment lay a golden ankh, wrought fine and gleaming, its surface alive with light. Snow lifted it with reverence. The metal was cool, yet seemed to pulse in her palm.

She drew it about her neck, and where it rested upon her breast she felt its weight and its warmth as though it had always belonged there.

The raven croaked once, low and solemn, and the silence deepened.

Snow rose and turned her steps toward the lagoon. Though the ruins were empty, she felt life pressing round her.

The ivy at her feet stirred, the stones seemed to thrum faintly beneath her tread. The air grew rich, heavy, filled with a sweetness too ancient to name. She felt herself hemmed in by a presence unseen—closer than breath, vaster than the sky, drawing her onward with a yearning that pierced bone and soul alike.

The path wound downward, guiding her into the great hollow. There the lagoon lay revealed in its fullness, circled by broken arches and fallen colonnades, shaped like a vast stadium. The waters glimmered as a second sky, and the ruins seemed to breathe as she entered their shadow.

From the far side of the lagoon she appeared. Bastet stepped forth among the ruins as though they had been raised for her alone.

Her head was that of the black cat, golden eyes burning with ancient fire. Her body shone perfect in its form—long legs, full curves, the elegance of womanhood carried with the grace of a huntress and the majesty of a queen. Her every stride was silence and command, the very air bending at her passage. The sistrum in her hand trembled faintly, and the soundless vibration quivered through the hollow like the echo of hidden music.

"I am Bastet," she said, her voice velvet and unbroken. It was not loud, yet it filled stone and water alike, seeping into the essence of Snow's flesh. "Protector and destroyer. Dancer of

33

truth. Enemy of masks. Enemy of crowns and false decrees. I am the raw pulse of the heart unbound."

Her golden eyes fixed upon Snow. "You chose well. Set offered his dominion, and you turned away. All who take his hand are severed from the Holy Land forever. But you—your pilgrimage remains. The road lies still before you."

Snow pressed her palm to the ankh at her breast. Her breath caught, her chest quivered, and Bastet's words burned in her like judgment and promise together.

The goddess turned to the lagoon. She waded forward, the waters parting for her as though they loved her. They slid across her bronze skin and clung to her heavenly attire without ripple or sound. Moonlight crowned her long limbs, and the ruins seemed to bow as she passed.

Her voice deepened, a hymn and a warning both. "Emotion is no weakness. It is truth unbound. Men bury fear, cloak grief, bind longing, and call it strength. Yet there is no strength in chains—only death. The sacred feminine rises when it ceases to hide. To feel, to rage, to weep, to laugh—this is power. This unmasks all falsehood. This is revelation."

She lifted the sistrum high, and the waters beneath her feet began to tremble. The sound was not heard but felt, a vibration rolling through the deep, swelling upward into the ruins. The lagoon quaked as though some great heart had begun to beat beneath it.

Bastet's black visage gleamed. "Snow, the waters remember what flesh has forgotten. Here waits the part of you that was torn away when you entered this broken world. In the beginning the soul was whole, but sin divided it—spirit from flesh, heart from truth. What you lost, you shall meet again."

The water swelled, rippling with light, and from the depths a shadow stirred. Long, sinuous, gliding like smoke yet heavy with strength. It rose higher, sleek and terrible—the Serpopard, half serpent, half leopard. Its scaled body writhed with power, its claws pressed lightly upon the surface as if it walked upon air. Its golden eyes burned, fixed upon Snow with a knowing that pierced deeper than sight.

It circled the lagoon, its movements fluid, its breath steady, the water bending itself to its command. Every ripple it left behind struck the stone like a drum, echoing in Snow's chest.

Bastet raised her hand, bracelets flashing. "Behold the Serpopard, Snow. This is no stranger. This is you. The part that wept when your lips were still. The part that raged when you were bound. The part that longed when you were denied. Wound and balm alike. This is your emotional spirit—the half stripped from you by sin, the half you were never meant to live without. And here, through dance, two shall be joined once more."

The waters pulsed louder, thrumming like a heart, and the beast bowed its long neck toward her—not in submission, but in recognition.

Snow's breath faltered. Her hand clutched the ankh against her breast. She knew, with a terror and longing she could not name, that she had reached the threshold.

***

The lagoon did not resist Bastet as she began to leave—it longed for her. The waters clung to her thighs, to her waist, to the swell of her hips as though unwilling to let go. When at last they slid free, they parted smooth as silk, falling in sheets that kissed her bronze skin. She rose from the depths like a vision born of moonlight and shadow, her long legs gleaming with the sheen of the divine, each step slow, measured, carrying with it the weight of something older than time. Her curves, unveiled and unashamed, swayed with elegance, her every movement a hymn to power and allure.

The sistrum rested in her hand, its frame glinting with liquid fire as droplets ran down its silver. She walked with the poise of a queen and the grace of a huntress, until she reached the fragment of marble shaped like a seat—waiting for her as if carved for no other purpose. She lowered herself upon it, long limbs folding with languid ease, her black visage gleaming, golden eyes alive with the fire of secrets.

Then came the sound—a sudden puff, soft as breath upon a mirror. The air thickened, the scent of cold night rushing in. From nothing he appeared: Khonshu, pale and tall, his cloak shimmering like woven shadow, his staff bright as if touched by fallen starlight. His eyes glowed like crescent moons—watchful, cunning, endless out of his falcon skull.

His lips curled into a smile, sly as a fox. "And here you are, radiant as ever, already settled in your throne. Were you truly going to begin without me, sister?" His tone was playful, but the edge beneath it could slice stone.

Bastet tilted her head, her long neck glistening in the silver wash of the moon. "Khonshu." Her voice rolled low, velvet and unhurried, like warm wine poured in silence. Her golden eyes fixed on him, unflinching, unbowed.

Khonshu feigned a wound, pressing a pale hand against his chest. "Do you not know how long I have awaited this night? The sky itself has grown restless with me. I would not miss such a dance—not for crowns nor empires, not for the flattery of kings. And to lend my hand to the most stunning of sisters—" His gaze roved across her form, pausing with deliberate slowness. His smile returned, sharp and wicked. "—that, I confess, is no burden at all."

A sound like a purr touched Bastet's throat, a low chuckle. She leaned ever so slightly, letting the light trace the curves of her body. "Tell me, Khonshu—do you ever take anything seriously?"

The mirth in his face shattered. His smile died like flame snuffed by wind. He straightened, tall and terrible, and the ruins themselves seemed to tighten at his sudden weight. His eyes narrowed, glowing white fire, and his voice rang out deep as a tolling bell.

"Do not mistake my jest for folly. The heavens bend upon my shoulders. I bear the scroll of night, the ledger of sorrow, the unbroken tide of death and birth. The stars obey my hand. The moon is my crown. There is none who takes more seriously what must be done."

At his words, the sky itself convulsed. The moon flared, bleeding red for a heartbeat. The stars swirled, their light falling in rivers of fire. The air quaked with the weight of his wrath, and the lagoon shuddered, waves striking the broken stone. Even the Serpopard stilled, golden eyes flashing toward him.

Yet Bastet did not cower. She sat unmoved, golden bracelets sliding along her wrist as she lifted one hand to rest lightly upon her thigh. Her lips curved into a slow, knowing smile, seductive as a blade drawn in candlelight.

"Good," she murmured, her voice silk and steel entwined. "It is about to begin."

From above, the raven swept down, wings stretched wide, gliding through the trembling air. It landed upon the pillar beside them, black feathers gleaming like polished obsidian. Bastet's fingers slid along its head with tender command, while Khonshu's severity softened into a sly grin. He caught the bird's gaze, and with a conspirator's ease, gave it a wink.

The lagoon lay waiting, its waters still thrumming. The Serpopard circled, slow and patient, as if it knew the hour had come.

***

Snow lingered at the rim of the lagoon, Bastet's words echoing still: *"It is about to begin."*

The waters shimmered before her, dark and deep, yet alive with mirrored stars. The Serpopard circled in silence, its golden eyes unblinking. Above, the heavens bent low, trembling with strange expectation. Her hand closed tight upon the ankh, her chest heaving, and doubt coiled round her like a serpent.

She drew back a step, fear pressing against her ribs. Was this to be judgment? Would she be found wanting?

And then—within, not without—a voice stirred. Gruff, rough-edged, like gravel under boot, yet steady as bedrock.

"Listen, girl."

Her breath caught. The ruins stood silent, the gods unmoved, the raven still. Yet the voice rumbled on, deeper than fear.

"They are not here to weigh you. Not here to condemn. Bastet, Khonshu, the beast in the water—all of them stand to witness. That's all. Witnesses to what must be done. To what you are about to reclaim."

Snow's brow furrowed, tears trembling in her eyes. The voice did not soften, but pressed harder, as though to hammer truth into her bones.

"This is not their trial. It's yours. And it's not punishment. It's freedom. They've gathered to see you reunited with yourself. To watch chains break. To bear witness to your liberation."

Her heart clenched. Something within her shifted, fragile yet fierce. She lowered her arms from where they clutched her chest, her shoulders rising with steadier breath.

The voice came once more, gravel and iron.

"Now step in, girl. Let them see you whole."

Snow lifted her chin. Her foot slid forward, touching the waters. Coolness wrapped her skin, not consuming but welcoming, as though the lagoon itself longed for her. She stepped again, deeper, until she stood within the mirrored heavens.

The Serpopard turned its long neck, golden eyes locking with hers. The gods remained still, the raven silent, yet she felt the truth of it—they were not her judges. They were her witnesses.

Snow drew another breath, deeper than the last, and stepped forward. The waters reached her knees, cool and weighty, yet they did not resist her. They seemed to open, folding round her legs, drawing her further in. Each step sank her deeper, until the mirrored sky rose about her waist, then her breast, until she stood in the very heart of the lagoon, bathed in the reflection of heaven.

The Serpopard circled, its golden eyes never leaving her, its sleek body coiling round the waters like a living shadow. It did not lunge, did not strike; it only waited, watching her with a gaze that demanded recognition.

Bastet rose from her seat. The goddess's long body unfolded with the elegance of a queen and the poise of a dancer. Her black feline visage gleamed against the silver sky, bracelets chiming faintly as she lifted the sistrum into her hand. She stepped forward, her voice velvet and commanding, seeping into every stone, every drop of water.

"Here begins the truth," she said. "The soul speaks not with words, but with the body. Fear, grief, longing, pride, courage, joy—these you have buried, and these you must awaken. You will not face them with sword nor crown. You will face them with dance. In this, the fracture will be healed."

She shook the sistrum once, and the sound cut like silver across the silence. The air quivered, the lagoon rippled, the Serpopard arched its neck, and the heavens above flickered as though stirred by unseen hands.

Snow's chest heaved, her hand pressed once more to the ankh at her breast. For a heartbeat, fear threatened to drag her under again.

Then the voice came—rough, steady, lodged within her.

"That's it, girl. You've stepped in. Don't falter now. Every beat of this dance is yours. And I'll be here. I'll see you through."

Snow's lips parted, trembling with tears she could not shed. The gruffness in the voice carried an edge she had never known—pride, raw and unguarded, breaking through stone.

The sistrum rattled again, sharper this time, and Bastet's golden eyes locked upon her.

"Now," said the goddess, her voice low and molten, "the dance begins."

The lagoon stirred, the sky shifted, the Serpopard drew closer. Bastet lifted her sistrum, and the sound rattled sharp, cutting the silence like iron on stone. Her voice rang through the hollow, velvet yet unyielding.

"Fear."

At once the heavens darkened, Khonshu raising his staff with a flick of his wrist. The sky turned navy, so deep it pressed upon the ruins like a weight. Lightning flared in sudden bursts, jagged spears tearing through the black. The light revealed Snow in fragments—face pale, body tense, breath shallow—then left her shrouded again in suffocating dark.

The waters responded, thrumming. The Serpopard drew near, circling her waist, its long body gliding across her chest as though to snare her. Snow's arms wrapped tight around herself, clutching her ribs, her movements stuttered and broken—jabbed steps, sudden twists, the frantic breath of a child. She staggered as though she stood once more at six years old, cowering beneath her bed, the world above filled with shadows that breathed.

Her knees buckled, her body hunched in on itself. Lightning split the sky again, casting the beast's golden eyes into sharp relief—so close they seemed to devour her.

Snow gasped. Her body folded tighter, as if the Serpopard's coils were crushing her lungs. The fear threatened to strangle her in her own skin.

Then came the voice—rough, deep, lodged within.

"Steady, girl."

She froze. The voice was unyielding, gravel and iron, but beneath it trembled something near to breaking.

"Don't let it choke you. Look at it. Face it. You've been here before, under that bed, heart pounding like a trapped bird. But you lived. You lived then, and you'll live now. Fear's only smoke."

Tears welled in her eyes, her arms loosening. The Serpopard pressed closer, its tail brushing her shoulders, its breath hot against her cheek.

Snow snapped her arms outward, sudden and jagged, breaking free for a moment. Her legs staggered, then stutter-stepped again, awkward and clinging.

Lightning tore the sky once more, Khonshu smirking as he flung a spear of white fire across the navy void. "Ahh," he murmured, voice echoing with mirth. "Even terror is art when the body quakes with it."

Snow shuddered, gasping, clutching her chest. The Serpopard coiled again, suffocating, yet she fought to stay upright, her movements broken but alive.

Grumpy's voice came again, rougher, louder.

"Good, lass. Breathe through it. Don't bow. Not to fear. Not ever."

Her eyes clenched shut. She hugged herself once more, then forced her arms outward, trembling, as though casting shadows off her flesh.

The lightning burned once more, then died. The navy sky sagged heavier, swallowing its own brilliance. The Serpopard hissed low, its coils loosening only to slide further into shadow. Snow's body still shook, arms trembling at her sides.

Bastet raised the sistrum again, her voice velvet and unyielding.

"Grief."

The word fell like stone into water. The lagoon sank into a purple abyss, thick and oppressive, its surface heavy as glass. The very air pressed down upon her lungs, and Snow's limbs followed—slack, dragging, lifeless.

Khonshu moved his staff in a slow circle, and the sky obeyed. Purple spread like bruising across the heavens, and ash rained down, glowing faintly before dying mid-air. His smile curled sharp. "Ah… grief. The weight that bends the spine, the sorrow that drinks the marrow. There is no fire so faithful."

Snow folded inward, clutching her ribs as though to keep herself from splitting. Her head pressed into her arms. Fourteen again, her body before the mirror draped in black, the mourner's veil heavy as chains. Her own reflection lost, her face hidden.

The Serpopard lowered itself with her, pressing its weight against her back. Its tail slid across her chest, pulling her into itself, demanding her collapse. Together they bent, twisted, bodies curled as though to hide from light.

Snow staggered, her steps dragging, her knees buckling. Each movement was a fall. Her arms shook, grasping at nothing, then wrapped around her chest again as though to bind the wound shut. Her face buried in shadow.

Then came the voice—rough, gruff, and sure.

"Don't vanish, lass. Not here. Grief'll swallow you whole if you let it."

She shook her head, her body rocking. The purple air thickened, choking her breath.

Grumpy's voice pressed harder, iron cutting through.

"I know it hurts. I know the loss feels endless. But grief isn't your grave, girl—it's the proof you loved, the proof you lived. Don't let it drown you. Breathe through it. Keep your head up."

Snow trembled, sagging against the Serpopard. It arched its long neck, brushing its muzzle beneath her chin, forcing her to lift her face from her arms. Her eyes streamed, her mouth open in a voiceless sob, but she raised her head.

The ash fell heavier, sticking to her wet cheeks. Still, she moved—awkward, ugly, but moving.

Bastet's golden eyes glimmered; she shook the sistrum once, its low hum resonating like a funeral bell.

Snow staggered, exhausted, her body already hollow from the weight. Her arms fell limp at her sides, her chest shaking with silent sobs.

Khonshu tilted his staff. The bruised sky thinned, lilac smoke bleeding in at the edges. It curled low, drifting like incense through the ruins, veiling the arches, creeping across the lagoon. The stars blurred, smothered in the haze.

Bastet lifted her sistrum, her voice low, mournful.

"Longing."

Snow's body slackened, puppet-like, her arms hanging, her gaze lost in the smoke. She was fifteen again, her hands pressed against the courtyard lattice, her eyes devouring the freedom beyond yet bound behind the bars.

Her body moved as if pulled by invisible strings—her arms rising weakly, trembling, only to drop again. The Serpopard circled her chest, its coils urging her upward, lifting her chin, but she sagged against it. Her knees buckled, her body folding limp as if she could sink into the water itself.

The lilac fog pressed closer, filling her mouth, her lungs, her soul. Snow's lips trembled, her chest heaving with voiceless cries. She bent forward, her tears streaming into the lagoon, her body slack as though she might dissolve into it.

Grumpy's voice rumbled, gravel and pride tangled.

"I know the ache, lass. The wanting that never ends. It'll drag you under if you let it. But don't mistake longing for death—it means you still hope, even when you curse it. Stand through it. Don't let it have you."

Snow sobbed, her hands reaching upward as though to grasp what the smoke concealed. Her body hung between collapse and ascent, the Serpopard's coils keeping her from drowning wholly.

Khonshu's smile softened, his eyes narrow, voice low. "Ah… longing. The sweetest torment. Desire without end. It devours more surely than sorrow."

Bastet did not look at him, her eyes burning gold. "It does not devour. It reveals."

Snow staggered forward, her body puppet-like, her arms limp yet lifted, her eyes hollow with hunger. The Serpopard circled tighter, its golden gaze locked upon her.

The lagoon shimmered beneath her, thick with smoke and tears.

The lilac fog shredded, its sorrow burnt away. In its place the sky flushed salmon pink, pulsing with a steady, royal beat. Khonshu twirled his staff and the heavens obeyed—bursts of light rose and fell like a drum, the stars forced into measured cadence. His mouth curled in sly amusement.

Bastet's sistrum chimed, sharp as metal. Her voice declared across the lagoon:

"Pride—false and vain."

Snow's spine straightened. Her chin rose, her shoulders squared. Her arms lifted into angular lines, her wrists rigid, her fingers poised as though holding unseen silk. Her steps slowed into gliding procession, heel pressed carefully to toe, as though she walked the polished floors of a royal hall.

She turned in sharp, measured angles, her arms extending outward as if to present herself to an invisible court. Each gesture carried dignity, yet no warmth—ceremony without heart.

The Serpopard mirrored her posture, circling with hauteur, its long neck arched, tail swaying with disdain. Together they performed the Allemande, moving in deliberate precision. Step, glide, turn; bow the head stiffly, then rise again. Their movements were beautiful, yet brittle as porcelain, regal as statues.

Snow's eyes flashed. She was twenty-one again, enthroned, her voice slicing the air in her Grand Decree, her words more law than mercy.

Khonshu raised his staff high, and the stars bent into the likeness of a crown of fire, descending to rest above her head. "Behold!" he laughed, his voice rolling with mock delight. "The sovereign of heaven, a queen crowned by the stars themselves!"

The crown burned bright, then shattered. Sparks rained down like embers, striking her shoulders and hair, scattering into the lagoon.

Snow faltered for an instant, fear flashing through her mask. Then she straightened again, lifting her arms high, stiffly twining her fingers with the Serpopard's coils as though she might command even the beast.

Grumpy's voice broke in, gruff, low, but with heat beneath it.

"Easy, lass. That crown's a noose if you cling too hard. Pride'll break your back quicker than fear or grief. Don't lose yourself to it."

Her body stiffened further, every gesture sharper, every step heavier. The Serpopard pressed close, eyes gleaming, as though waiting for her to crack.

Bastet's golden gaze narrowed, the sistrum rattling low. "False crowns always tremble. Masks cannot endure."

And then—without warning—the salmon light softened. Teal rose within it, pulsing through the sky like lanterns in the night. Khonshu lowered his staff, and the stars shimmered not as embers but as threads of silver, weaving gently into the heavens.

Bastet's voice warmed, velvet and resonant. "Pride—true and pure."

Snow's posture broke. Her stiff arms lowered, her steps loosened, and the rigid Allemande melted into something freer, lighter. Her spine curved, her movements softened into fluidity. Her legs extended long and graceful, her feet pressing light against the water as though she skimmed across it.

She twirled, spinning not for ceremony but for joy. Her arms lifted, loose now, her hands open, her body no longer a statue but a dancer.

The Serpopard's arrogance faded with hers. It circled low and steady, its body fluid, its head lowered in harmony rather than disdain. Together they turned, no longer rigid partners but companions.

Snow's eyes lifted. She was twenty-one still, but not enthroned. She stood among her people, the village light glowing around her, their faces warm in the fire's glow. Pride not of decree, but of belonging.

Grumpy's voice cracked faintly as it rumbled through her mind.

"There now, lass. That's it. That's the pride worth keeping. Not the crown, but the bond. Hold fast to that one."

Her movements grew fuller, her arms rising wide, her legs gliding across the lagoon with grace. The teal light pulsed, and the silver threads fell from the heavens, weaving into her form as though stitching her back together.

Bastet's lips curved faintly, her voice low as she shook the sistrum. "Yes… this is the pride that stands."

The lagoon shimmered with teal and salmon, the yin and yang of false and true, crown and bond, one fading into the other.

The teal sky shimmered, then bled. Maroon spread like fire through the heavens, pulsing in swirls that curved and twisted. Khonshu lifted his staff and the stars above flared brighter, scattering like sparks from a forge.

Bastet shook the sistrum once, the sound sharper, more insistent. Her golden eyes burned as she spoke.

"Courage."

The waters quaked, rippling outward in waves. Snow's steps shifted—no longer graceful. Her feet stamped, sending bursts across the surface. Her arms cut through the air, deliberate, fierce. She was twenty-five again, standing before the gates engulfed in flame, heat searing her face, her heart trembling but her body unyielding.

The Serpopard leapt beside her, its muscles taut, its claws striking the water with each blow. It lunged and parried with her, as if locked in combat with unseen foes. Together they struck and spun, their limbs extended, their bodies taut with strength. Each movement was a duel—thrust, deflect, strike, recover.

Snow's breath grew ragged, her muscles trembling, but she pressed forward. Her arms extended fully, her steps hammered the lagoon as though she would break the water itself.

Khonshu leaned forward, his pale eyes gleaming, his voice sharp. "Yes! Strike! Show the night you will not be broken!" He flung his staff high, and a comet seared across the maroon sky, blazing a fiery path that split the heavens.

Bastet's voice deepened, velvet with fire. "Do not falter, Snow. Let the strength of your spirit drive you. Show us the flame that fear could not quench."

Snow lunged, the Serpopard beside her, their forms a mirror of ferocity. She swung her arms outward, her muscles taut, her face resolute. The beast's tail lashed with hers, water bursting in arcs of light.

Grumpy's voice thundered inside her chest, breaking rougher than before. "That's it, lass! Show them your mettle! Show them what's been forged in you! You've carried more than fire and gates—carry this!"

Snow roared, her voice breaking free for the first time, raw and primal. Her body arched back, then slammed forward, her arms outstretched, her legs driving through the water. The Serpopard matched her with perfect fury, its claws raking, its neck striking forward.

The stars above swirled faster, the maroon sky ablaze with light. Khonshu's laughter rang sharp, delighted. "Look at her, Bastet! She fights as though the heavens themselves bend to her will!"

Bastet's lips curved in rare approval, her sistrum shaking with urgency. "She does not fight alone. She fights whole."

Snow's body burned with strength, her movements fierce, unrelenting. Courage surged through her, and the lagoon itself seemed to quake with her steps.

The maroon sky swirled, blazing with fire and fury—then softened. From the edges of heaven, mint green spilled in, shimmering, light as dew upon morning grass. The comet faded, replaced by stars that twinkled bright, playful, alive.

Bastet lifted her sistrum high, and its rattle sang bright and ringing. Her voice rang across the ruins:

"Joy."

Snow's body shifted. The stamp of her feet lightened, her arms extended wide, her chest opening to the sky. Her legs leapt, her steps glided. The water splashed about her, not as battle, but as laughter.

She was thirty-three again, in the wildflower meadow, the grass high, the blossoms brushing her skin, the air filled with the sweetness of earth and sun. She twirled with abandon, her laughter spilling, her arms flung wide, her heart unbound.

The Serpopard bounded with her, no longer a shadow or burden, but a companion in play. Its long body curved in graceful arcs, leaping through the waters with her, mirroring her spins and turns. Together they glided, free and fearless, two halves reunited in delight.

Snow's mouth opened, and laughter escaped her lips—bright, ringing, startling even to her own ears.

Khonshu leapt to his feet, his staff raised, his voice breaking into sharp joy. "Yes! Yes! Let her laugh, Bastet! Let the heavens hear it!" He flung his arms wide, and the stars burst into showers, streaks of green and silver cutting through the night sky like fireworks.

Bastet rose too, her golden eyes burning, her voice velvet but unrestrained. "Dance, Snow! Dance with the fullness of your heart! This is what was stolen from you—claim it back!" Her sistrum rang furiously, a rhythm fierce with celebration.

Grumpy's voice thundered within her, gruff but shaking with pride. "That's it, lass! That's the one! You've carried fear, you've carried grief, but joy—joy is yours. Don't let go of it now. Don't ever let it go!"

Snow leapt, her arms outstretched, her body fully extended, the lagoon spraying light with every bound. The Serpopard twined beside her, their motions no longer jagged or strained, but seamless, jubilant. They spun, they leapt, they glided, laughter filling the hollow as though creation itself rejoiced.

The heavens above twinkled faster, mint-green fire showering the sky. Khonshu laughed aloud, fierce and unrestrained. Bastet's sistrum shook until the ruins themselves seemed to vibrate. The raven gave a single loud cry, wings beating against the pillar.

Snow twirled once more, her hair flung wide, her body radiant with freedom. For the first time, she felt it—she was whole.

The mint-green brilliance of joy still clung to her limbs, but then the heavens convulsed. Khonshu threw his staff high, and the sky obeyed with fury and wonder.

"Now!" he cried, his voice cracking the silence like thunder. "Now—my favorite part!"

The heavens burst open. Every color of the trial ignited at once—the navy of fear, the purple abyss of grief, the lilac haze of longing, the salmon and teal of pride, the maroon fire of courage, the mint of joy—all of them collided and swirled, weaving into rivers of color across the night. Lightning slashed, stars twinkled, comets burned, fog drifted, auroras

swam—all in one vast, uncontainable harmony. The lagoon mirrored it, doubling the glory until it seemed Snow danced within two heavens, above and below.

Snow's body broke open in movement. No longer bound by form, no longer crushed by sorrow, she flung her arms wide, spun with abandon, leapt with every ounce of her being. Her tears streamed in torrents, downpouring across her cheeks, her chest heaving with sobs of joy. She laughed through them, cried through them, her body free in every limb.

The Serpopard danced with her, its coils fluid, its leaps radiant, their forms bound in perfect unison. Each turn, each bound, their movements dissolved into one another, until it was no longer Snow and the beast, but one spirit split into two forms preparing to be joined.

Grumpy's voice rose, rougher, thicker, breaking with emotion. "By God... girl, it's beautiful. All of it. To see you whole, to see you free—what an honor it's been... to be part of your story."

Snow fell to her knees in the water, arms raised high, her body shaking with sobs, her face lifted to the storm of light.

Khonshu's voice thundered over the ruins, over the lagoon, over heaven itself. "Look! Look, you stars! Look, you heavens! Bear witness! Here is a creation—torn, complex, broken, and yet beautiful! She has walked through shadow, she has carried chains, and now—now she returns whole! Bear witness to the daughter who dances her way home!" His voice rang with the cadence of a preacher on fire, every word filled with joy, with praise, with holy madness. "God of the heavens—look upon her! See what has been reclaimed!"

The stars blazed brighter, as though the whole cosmos applauded. Comets streaked in chorus, meteors fell like rain.

Snow screamed with laughter and tears, her arms spread, her body spinning in the riot of light. And in that instant the Serpopard lunged—not in fury, but in union. Its long neck arched, its golden eyes burning, and it dove straight into her chest.

The water exploded in silver light. Snow gasped, every limb shuddering, her body flung back as though struck—but then stilled. The lagoon calmed, the heavens held their breath.

She opened her eyes. Her chest rose. Her tears streamed still, but her face shone with peace. The Serpopard was gone—not vanished, but within, her spirit and her body one again.

Bastet lowered her sistrum, silent tears tracing her bronze cheeks, golden eyes unblinking. She bowed her head slightly, not in pity but in reverence.

Snow knelt in the water, arms open, face lifted to the sky, weeping freely, radiant, whole.

She was free.

Trial 3: The Gate of Becoming

"Let each of you look not only to his own interests, but also

to the interests of others."

Philippians 2:4

The lagoon still clung to her lashes in silver droplets, the echo of Khonshu's blessing pulsing faintly in her chest. She drew in a long, steady breath, letting the cool air fill her lungs, as if she might carry a fragment of the waters with her.

When she opened her eyes again—

The world had changed.

The soft shimmer of the lagoon was gone. Before her stretched a barren wasteland, endless and gray, its horizon choked in dust. The earth was cracked and lifeless, yet it groaned with memory, as though beneath the dead soil something ancient still stirred. The air tasted of ash and silence, stripped of song and color.

And then she saw him.

Aker, the eternal guardian of time, rose from the wasteland like a living monument. His form was vast, leonine yet cosmic, a colossal being with two heads—one gazing eternally into the Past, the other fixed upon the Future. Their golden eyes burned like twin suns, unblinking, merciless in their watch. His body was half buried in the earth itself, as though he *was* the horizon, anchoring the passage of ages with his very flesh. Between his paws lay a narrow passage of shadow, a gate Snow knew instinctively no soul could cross without reckoning.

Before she could steady her breath, another presence stirred.

Sekhmet.

She appeared quietly beside Aker, though her arrival shifted the air as though fire had entered the wasteland. Snow had read tales of her, but no words had ever conjured the sight that now stood before her. She was terrible and magnificent—a lioness-headed goddess, her mane a crown of flame, her eyes searing with the heat of suns. Gold armor clung to her like a second skin, polished not by hand but by blood and reverence, every plate engraved with prayers long faded from mortal tongues. In her hand she held no weapon, for she was herself the embodiment of war and healing, destruction and restoration.

The Raven sat perched upon her shoulder, black feathers stark against her burning presence. It tilted its head, silent, as though recording each breath of this moment into the memory of eternity.

Snow did not speak. She only stood, heart beating hard in her chest, and *observed*.

Sekhmet's gaze fell upon Snow, heavy as the desert sun, yet not cruel. Her voice, when it came, rumbled like a furnace, low and resonant, as though carried on the breath of ages.

"Snow of the white skin," she said, "you stand now at the Gate of Becoming. Here no crown will shield you, no grief will excuse you, no triumph will exalt you. I am not your judge. I am your mirror. And in my fire, you will not be condemned—you will *see*."

She lifted a clawed hand, and the air between them shimmered like heat above the sand. Images flickered—faces, places, small forgotten deeds glimmering like sparks in the void.

"You believe yourself the center, the thread upon which all hangs. But I will show you how every life, every choice, every root and feather and stone, is bound to yours. This is no trial of guilt nor innocence. It is a passage of reflection and understanding. Your task is to *listen*. To watch. To weigh the lives you thought insignificant, and to recognize their weight in the weaving of your own."

Sekhmet's burning eyes narrowed.

"Do you understand?"

Snow swallowed hard, her throat dry with dust, and bowed her head. "I do," she whispered.

For a moment, the wasteland was still. Then the Raven clicked its beak, a sharp sound like the snapping of a quill against parchment, as if sealing the oath.

Sekhmet inclined her head, satisfied. "Good. You will not walk this lesson alone."

She turned slightly, and from the shadow of Aker's vast body stepped a small figure. Bashful. His presence was soft, almost swallowed by the wasteland's immensity, yet Snow felt

51

a wave of quiet comfort rise at the sight of him. His eyes, shy and gentle, met hers for only an instant before he lowered them again. He did not speak—he would never speak—but the weight of his silence was an anchor, a reminder that even the unnoticed carried immeasurable worth.

"Here is your familiar," Sekhmet said. "He will not guide, he will not instruct. He will only be. Learn from his stillness. Learn from his place in the whole."

Snow nodded once, her heart steadied by his presence.

Sekhmet's gaze swept across the wasteland, and even the dust seemed to still at her words.

"Before we begin," she said, "you must understand the weight of *three*. It is no idle number, no accident of counting. Three is the measure of wholeness—the weaving of beginning, middle, and end. It is the balance of past, present, and future. It is the triad that binds creation to destruction and destruction to renewal. Without three, nothing endures."

Her lioness eyes burned brighter, twin suns glaring from a single face.

"You have passed through one gate, then another. And now you stand at the third. This is no coincidence. For here you must learn that your story is not only yours. Three reminds us that no life is singular—every thread is bound to others. Each tale you dismissed, each soul you deemed unworthy, is part of your weave. You cannot cut them away without cutting yourself."

Snow lowered her head, the truth of it settling into her chest like a heavy stone.

Sekhmet leaned closer, her mane glowing like embers against the wasteland gloom. "Three asks of you this: will you see the whole, or will you continue to believe you alone are center? Today, you must learn that every story matters—no matter how small, no matter how forgotten."

The Raven shifted on her shoulder, feathers rustling like the turning of a page.

Sekhmet's burning eyes narrowed, her voice dropping lower, as though she were dragging the truth up from the bones of the earth.

"Tell me, Snow… do you remember the Huntsman?"

Snow's breath caught in her throat.

"The one commanded to take you into the forest," Sekhmet continued, "to press his blade into your flesh, to carve from you your lungs and your liver. The feast of proof for a jealous Queen."

The wasteland air seemed to thicken around them, heavy with the echo of that command long past. The Raven tilted its head, black eyes glinting. Bashful's hands folded before him, silent but steady, as though bracing Snow for what she was about to see.

Sekhmet's gaze held her fast.

"Do you remember him, child?"

Sekhmet lifted her hand, and the wasteland rippled. The dust rose, whirling into shapes, until the gray plain gave way to the edge of a dark forest. Trees loomed, their branches clawing at the sky, and there stood the Huntsman.

He was as Snow remembered—broad-shouldered, his face creased with both strength and fear. In his grip trembled a hunting knife, its steel catching the dim light like a serpent's fang. His chest heaved as though each breath might betray him.

Snow gasped. She *knew* this place. She could feel again the chill of the forest, the pounding terror in her child's heart. She watched herself—a younger Snow, pale and trembling—fall to her knees before him.

The Huntsman raised his blade, lips pressed into a grim line. But his eyes... his eyes betrayed him. They glistened with pity, with horror at the command he'd been given.

"Run," he whispered, his voice raw, desperate. "Go, child. Run, and never look back."

The younger Snow fled into the shadows, her small figure vanishing among the trees.

But the Huntsman did not turn home empty-handed. His body shuddered as he forced himself deeper into the wood. There, with trembling hands, he seized a wild boar. The animal squealed and fought, but soon its life spilled into the earth. With gritted teeth, he carved from it the organs demanded—the lungs, the liver—blood steaming in the cold air.

He fell to his knees, clutching the grisly tokens. His lips moved soundlessly, a prayer or perhaps a curse. Then, with hollow eyes, he turned back toward the castle, bearing his false offering.

The wasteland snapped back around them. The image dissolved into dust, leaving only silence and the echo of iron on bone.

Sekhmet's voice broke the stillness.

"He spared you, yes. But what did you believe became of him when you walked away?"

The dust stirred again, pulling Snow forward into another vision.

Now the Huntsman stood in a great hall, stone walls hung with blackened banners. His shoulders were bowed, his eyes hollow, yet a trembling relief quivered in him—for the Queen had summoned him not with wrath, but with reward.

Before him, servants laid a golden platter. Steam rose from it, rich and savory. Upon it lay roasted meat, glistening in its juices. The Queen, clad in her cruel majesty, smiled with serpentine delight.

"Eat, loyal one," she purred, her voice dripping with poisoned sweetness. "Feast, for your service is most pleasing to me."

The Huntsman's hands shook as he lifted the fork, piercing the tender flesh. He did not question—he *dared not*. He ate.

And the Queen laughed.

Her voice split the hall like thunder, her teeth bared in triumph.

"You dine upon your own blood. Your wife, your daughters—you consume what you thought to protect."

The platter blurred, the meat twisting in Snow's sight until she saw their faces—his beloved family, eyes wide and empty, consumed by the man who had betrayed his Queen's command.

The Huntsman gagged, retching, but the Queen's guards seized him, forcing him back upon his knees.

The vision shifted.

Now it was the village square, crowded with faces. Snow smelled the iron tang of fear and smoke. The Huntsman was bound upon the scaffold, his body broken by chains. The Queen's decree rang out:

"Let all see the fate of traitors, who dare to place mercy above obedience."

The executioner raised his axe, glinting beneath the gray sky. With a single stroke, the Huntsman's head fell, rolling across the cobblestones. Gasps, screams, silence. His blood pooled dark, soaking into the earth where children once played.

The memory shattered. The wasteland returned.

Sekhmet's eyes fixed on Snow, unrelenting.

"This is the weave you never saw. You lived because he spared you. And he died because he did."

The Raven cawed once, sharp and echoing, like a gavel striking judgment.

The wasteland's silence lingered, heavy as stone. Snow's chest heaved, her lips trembling though no words escaped.

Sekhmet's voice cut through, low and steady.

"Tell me, Snow… after he spared you, did you ever inquire of this man? Did you ever wonder what became of him? Did you even *think* of him once your feet had carried you to safety?"

Snow closed her eyes. The answer seared her tongue, bitter as ash. "No," she whispered. "I did not."

The goddess inclined her head, her lion eyes burning. "And how old were you, child? Barely more than a girl. Do you believe you were truly capable of thinking beyond yourself?"

Snow's breath caught. She wanted to protest, to defend—but the truth pressed heavy. In the shadows of that moment, she had thought of nothing but her own beating heart, her own desperate escape.

Sekhmet stepped closer, her mane flickering like embers in the dark.

"In a life and death struggle, how do we decide whose life is worth dying for? The hunted child, or the man who held the blade? What measure decides who may live, and who must fall? Such questions haunt every story. Such choices shape every fate."

Snow bowed her head, her heart a storm of guilt and grief. Bashful stirred beside her, his silence a quiet balm, as though reminding her that the weight of these questions was not hers alone to bear.

Sekhmet let the silence stretch, letting Snow's reflection root deep. Then, at last, she turned her gaze toward the horizon.

"Come," she said. "There are more stories to face."

Sekhmet raised her hand once more, and the wasteland stirred like a page turning. The dust coiled and thickened until it birthed another memory, faint and flickering as candlelight.

Snow found herself standing upon a narrow village path. The cottages were poor and sagging, their roofs patched with straw, smoke rising thinly into the gray sky. Chickens scattered at the hem of a girl's skirt. She was young—perhaps no older than Snow herself had been when the Huntsman spared her. Her dress was threadbare, patched a dozen times, her hands calloused from toil.

Yet there was a brightness in her eyes, a trembling kind of awe, as she whispered to the stranger who stood before her. A man with noble bearing, clad in fine clothes, though dust and

wear marked the road upon him. Snow's breath caught—she knew this man. The one who would later be called her "Prince."

The girl leaned closer, her voice hushed.

"They say she lies in a coffin of glass," she murmured, glancing about as though the very trees might betray her words. "A coffin guarded by seven small men, who will not bury her because she is too beautiful for the earth to claim. She sleeps as though alive, an angel, untouched by rot."

The nobleman's eyes widened, wonder flooding his face. Without this whisper, without the trembling courage of a poor peasant child, he would never have known where to look.

Snow pressed a hand to her chest. She remembered none of this. She had lain in death's mimicry, trapped in enchanted silence, while this girl had unwittingly set the course of her return.

The vision blurred. The nobleman hurried away, led by the girl's words. She watched him go, her bare feet rooted in the dust of her village street, unknowing that in a single breath she had altered the weave of queens and kingdoms.

Sekhmet's voice echoed from above the scene, stern yet weighted with truth.

"This one you never thanked. This one you never knew. Yet without her, your coffin would have lain hidden until time consumed even the stone around it. Tell me, Snow—was she insignificant?"

The image began to dissolve, the girl's small frame swallowed by the wasteland dust, leaving Snow with the question burning in her chest.

Snow's breath faltered, her hand pressed tight against her chest.

"I… never thought," she whispered. "Never even wondered if someone had led him. He never spoke of a girl. He told me only that he found me wandering—drawn by chance, by fate. I believed him. I never questioned…"

Her voice trailed into silence, the truth curdling bitter on her tongue. The Raven gave a low, throaty croak, as though mocking her realization.

Sekhmet's eyes glowed like twin coals in the dust.

"Tell me, child—has your king never lied to you? Has he never taken what was not his, and named it his own? Then why are you surprised? Why are you wounded to learn he claimed the glory of your discovery alone?"

Snow bowed her head, shame flooding her cheeks. The memory of his words echoed— his certainty, his proud retelling of how he had 'stumbled upon her coffin by fate's design.' How easily she had believed. How little she had thought to question.

The image of the peasant girl lingered in her mind—eyes wide, voice trembling, a spark of courage no one had seen fit to remember. A girl who had altered kingdoms, and been erased from the telling.

Sekhmet's mane shimmered in the wasteland's gloom, her voice like fire wrapping iron.

"This is the truth you must swallow: stories are stolen, and names forgotten. You rose because another whispered. He did not wander alone. And yet she vanished from the tale, while he wore the crown of discovery."

Snow closed her eyes, a tear sliding unbidden down her cheek. She whispered, barely audible, "I never even thought to ask his steps. I never thought to ask who came before him."

The dust stirred, restless, waiting for the future to be shown.

Snow's tear fell into the dust, vanishing as though the wasteland itself devoured it.

Her lips parted, trembling, words forming in her throat—"If only I had—"

But Sekhmet's hand rose, silencing her. Her voice came like molten iron, burning away protest.

"No."

The lioness goddess leaned closer, her eyes twin suns that allowed no shadow of self-pity.

"You are not here to wish. You are not here to rewrite. You are here to *see*. Reflection, not revision, is the path of this gate. Do you understand?"

Snow swallowed, her heart pounding. She nodded.

Sekhmet's mane flared with heat, her voice like the roar of a furnace.

"Yes, it is bitter. Yes, it wounds your pride to realize how easily you were deceived, how foolishly you trusted. But hear me, child: the fool is not worthless. The fool is *necessary*. The fool plays their role upon the stage so that the rest may move into place. Without the fool's steps, the play collapses. Without error, there is no awakening."

The Raven clicked its beak once, sharp as a quill scoring parchment.

"Hold fast to this truth," Sekhmet said. "You are not meant to *fix* what was. You are meant to listen, to see how all threads connect. Even those of the fool. Even those of the forgotten."

Snow drew a shuddering breath, the sting in her chest easing, though the wound still bled within. Bashful, silent and steady, stood a little closer at her side, his very presence a balm against the weight of shame.

Sekhmet straightened, her eyes shifting again to the horizon of dust.

"Now, see what became of the girl who carried a kingdom with a whisper."

The wasteland began to stir again.

The dust swirled again, and the village reformed before Snow's eyes—but it was no longer the place of whispers and smoke curling gently from chimneys.

The sky was red, not with sunset but with flame. Ash drifted like snowflakes. Screams pierced the air, sharp as broken glass.

The cottages burned. Whole thatched roofs collapsed into embers, beams splitting, sparks spiraling upward like the souls of the condemned. Soldiers moved through the smoke, their armor glinting, torches raised high. Behind them loomed the banners of a fractured church, their edges blackened by the very fire they carried.

Snow's gaze fell to the girl—no longer a child, but worn thin by poverty, her eyes ringed with despair. She clutched a bundle to her chest, though it was not gold or grain, only scraps of cloth, the last remnants of her family's life. Around her, neighbors were dragged into the street. Some wept, others cursed, but all were broken beneath the decree: *their property seized, their lives consumed in the name of holy reform.*

The girl stumbled, coughing in the smoke, watching her home collapse in flames. She tried to speak—Snow saw her lips move, forming words swallowed by the roar of fire. But no one heard. No one listened. She was erased, not by blade or poison, but by indifference and the slow grind of history.

Then the vision stilled, locked in a single image: the peasant girl on her knees in the ash, her hands lifted as though in supplication—not to be spared, but simply to be *seen.*

Sekhmet's voice cut through the smoke, harsh but steady. "She whispered once, and a kingdom shifted. She was erased once, and the world did not notice. Such is the weight of stories. Even the smallest voice can alter the fate of queens… and yet even that voice may vanish without remembrance."

The Raven cawed, the sound sharp and merciless, like the tearing of parchment.

The vision broke. The wasteland returned, gray and barren, but the stench of smoke seemed to linger still in Snow's lungs.

Sekhmet turned to her, eyes burning.

"Do you see now? Nothing is insignificant. All threads matter to the weave. Even the ones burned, forgotten, and unnamed."

Snow's chest still burned with the smoke of the village when Sekhmet's voice rose again, low and resonant, like wind through a crypt.

"Yes," she said, her lion's eyes glinting. "And now you must see through the eyes of what few acknowledge as life at all."

The wasteland trembled, its dust swirling at her command. "You think only people shape the tale? You think only kings and peasants, huntsmen and brides, weigh upon the weave? Foolish child. Even the earth breathes upon your story. Even the trees bend their boughs to shape your steps. And you, in turn, have carved your will upon them."

The Raven shifted on her shoulder, feathers glistening like ink spilled across a page. Its black eye seemed to fix Snow with a knowing glare.

Sekhmet's mane rippled like fire in the desert wind as she spoke:

"The plants you pass, the stones you cut, the rivers you drink—they are not passive ornaments in your tale. They are your companions, your witnesses, your victims. They remember every footprint you have pressed into their skin. As you direct them, so too do they direct you. Without their root, you would starve. Without their timber, you would sleep in cold. And without their mine, your kingdom would have rotted into ruin."

Her words lingered, sharp as iron. "Now, look, and see what the forest bore for you."

She spread her hand, and the wasteland quivered, dissolving into shadowed trees. Their trunks gleamed faintly, as though veins of gemstone pulsed within them. The air shimmered with unseen magic, alive with whispers.

Snow's breath caught. She knew these woods. She could feel the heart of the Enchanted Forest, alive and ancient, watching her even now.

The vision swelled, and Snow felt herself dissolve into the forest.

Her feet sank into rich earth, damp and breathing. Her arms stretched high, and they were not arms at all, but branches—broad and strong, crowned with green, swaying in the hidden music of the wind. Beneath her canopy, weary wanderers found shade. Birds stitched songs into her boughs, and the small creatures of the wood darted safely through her roots.

She was *tree*—not apart from them, but one of them. She could feel the heartbeat of the forest pulsing up through her trunk, the slow, eternal rhythm of roots drinking deep, of leaves drinking light. Every vein of stone that glittered beneath the soil thrummed with living magic, old as the first dawn.

Sekhmet's voice threaded through the rustle of leaves.

"In your past, you found here a gift. Beneath these roots, a mine of gemstone—garnet, amethyst, sapphire—poured forth its riches. You, Snow, introduced this treasure to your people. From it, your kingdom rose again after the Queen's fall. You believed it salvation."

Snow shuddered, her branches trembling. She remembered the coffers filled, the hunger that waned, the new roads laid in stone. She had thought it mercy. She had thought it wise.

But the forest pulsed beneath her, a reminder that nothing is given without price.

The air glowed with magic, soft as a hymn. She felt it in her bark, in her sap, in the crown of her leaves: life abundant, protection freely given.

Yet, faint at the edges of her knowing, there was a shadow—a gnawing echo of what was still to come. A taste of iron, of ash, of the axe biting into living flesh.

Snow drew in a breath, branches rattling like bones in a crypt.

She knew what Sekhmet would show next.

The glow of the forest dimmed. The air that once shimmered with unseen song curdled into silence.

Snow gasped—her branches cracked. Once-green leaves withered into brittle husks, snapping from her boughs like falling ash. Her roots, once sunk deep in nourishing soil, now writhed in stone and emptiness. The earth beneath her had been hollowed, torn open by greedy hands.

She felt it all.

The axes biting into her bark were blades in her flesh. The shovels that gutted the mines were claws raking through her muscles. Each gemstone torn from the earth was not wealth, but lifeblood ripped from her veins.

The voices of her fellow trees keened in the wind, not in song but in despair. Birds no longer nested in her boughs—only black smoke curled upward, choking the sky. The streams that once sang turned black with silt, their waters sluggish, poisoned.

Snow cried out, though the sound was not with her lips but with her cracking trunk. She could feel herself collapsing, hollowed, a carcass of what had been. The magic that once danced bright as stars within the roots flickered, flickered—then bled into darkness.

Sekhmet's voice rang, steady and merciless, through the agony.

"This is the future you set in motion. You thought you healed your kingdom, but you fed its hunger with the forest's bones. And if nothing changes, this is the end: silence, rot, and magic ground into dust."

The Raven's wings spread wide, feathers falling like black snow.

Snow felt her last leaf crumble to dust, her branches clawing upward in vain supplication. She was tree, she was land, she was death.

Then, with a wrenching snap, the vision shattered.

Snow stumbled back into her own body, gasping, the wasteland reasserting itself around her. Yet the ache of broken roots lingered deep within her chest.Her breath trembled, but her eyes no longer fled from the truth Sekhmet had laid bare.

She whispered, voice raw:

"It is not for me to be the savior of this tale. I was never meant to mend all wounds, nor carry the end in my hands. My task was only to lay the stones of the path… to begin what another must finish. Someone will come—someone whose story will rise from mine, who will right what I have wronged."

Her words grew steadier, conviction sharpening like steel. "Yes. This will be fixed. It must be. I believe it."

Her gaze lifted to Sekhmet, and for the first time there was no plea in her eyes, only the solemn weight of acceptance. The Raven shifted on the goddess's shoulder, tilting its head as though acknowledging the truth. Bashful, still silent, gave the faintest nod, his presence warm and steady beside her.

Sekhmet's fiery mane rippled, her eyes unreadable.

At last, she inclined her head—the faintest gesture, but one that seemed to set the wasteland itself at ease, as though the earth had exhaled.

Snow's heart pounded, not with pride but with a deeper rhythm, one that hummed in time with the weave of all things. For the first time, she understood: her story was not the story. She was a thread in the tapestry, and another hand would take up the pattern where hers faltered.

Sekhmet extended her hand, clawed yet radiant, the fire of her mane softening to a steady glow. Snow hesitated only a heartbeat before placing her pale hand in the goddess's grasp. The warmth that surged through her was fierce but not consuming, a fire that steadied instead of scorched.

Together they walked across the barren wasteland toward the looming bulk of Aker. The twin lion heads regarded her still, one gazing backward into the Past, the other unblinking toward the Future. Their golden eyes burned, merciless yet eternal.

As they drew near, Sekhmet's voice rose, strong as thunder, yet laced with an undertone of reverence.

"Snow of the white skin," she said, "you have seen the weave. The Huntsman's mercy, the Peasant's whisper, the Forest's silent sacrifice—all bound to your story, and you bound to theirs. This is the truth you must carry: when you believe yourself the main character, when you clutch the tale to your chest as though it were yours alone, you step out of alignment with the Whole. And when you fall from alignment, the world does not punish you—it merely mirrors your brokenness. The cosmos itself recoils when one strand of the pattern seeks to be the loom."

Her golden eyes softened, if only slightly.

"But today, you have learned. You have seen. You understand you are not the end, only the beginning. And that wisdom is no small triumph. Few pass this gate without crumbling beneath pride or despair. But you stand."

The Raven spread its wings, loosing a single cry that echoed like the tolling of a bell across the barren plain. Bashful's silent gaze shone with quiet pride.

Before them, Aker stirred. The earth trembled as the twin lions groaned and shifted, their colossal forms arching skyward. Their bodies, once sunk deep into the soil, pulled free, curving together until they formed a vast archway. Stone and sinew intertwined, glowing faintly with the light of ages. Between them, the empty wasteland split open into a radiant threshold.

Sekhmet released Snow's hand, turning to face her one last time. Her mane blazed in the dim air, a crown of holy flame.

"You have done well, child. You have reached the third gate. Take pride not in your might, but in your humility, in your wisdom. For only through this have you earned the passage."

Snow gazed into the archway. Within it churned not light nor land, but swirling darkness—chaotic, formless, raw. It seethed like a storm before the first dawn, a void before creation itself. The sight clawed at her mind, promising madness and revelation alike.

Sekhmet's voice lowered, almost tender.

"Beyond Aker lies that which existed before all order—the Chaos that was before creation. Step with care, Snow. You will need every truth you have gathered to endure what waits there."

Snow drew in a final breath of the wasteland air, its dust still bitter on her tongue. Her hand lingered at her chest where Sekhmet's warmth had steadied her, but now she stood alone before the arch of Aker.

The twin lion-heads groaned low, ancient voices rumbling like shifting mountains, and the threshold yawned wider. Beyond it churned a darkness deeper than any night—a storm of shadows without form, a seething void that writhed as though it were alive. It was not silence but the soundless roar of everything unmade, the Chaos that preceded creation.

Snow stepped forward.

At once, the ground dissolved beneath her feet. The wasteland, Sekhmet's burning gaze, even Bashful's quiet comfort—all fell away. She was swallowed whole, body and soul, into the abyss.

The void clutched at her with unseen hands, pulling her in every direction. Her breath tore ragged from her throat, and still she forced her eyes open. Shapes shifted in the dark: serpents of shadow, coils of light half-born, fragments of things that might be stars but not yet.

And then—

The Raven.

Its wings flashed black against the storm, beating strong as it cut ahead of her into the Chaos. For a moment Snow felt relief, her heart leaping at the sight of her silent witness.

But the Raven did not return.

It soared further, further still, until its dark feathers were swallowed by the void, vanishing utterly from her sight.

Snow reached out, but her hand met only emptiness. The truth settled cold upon her: she must face what lay beyond this gate alone. No guide. No mirror. No comfort. Only the raw, untamed Chaos, waiting to test her soul.

The darkness closed around her, vast and endless.

And the fourth trial began.

Trial 4: The Cry of Innocence

"My God, my God, why have you forsaken me?"

Matthew 27:46

Snow stepped beyond the archway Aker had become, and the moment she crossed, Sekhmet's hand slipped from hers. The light of the last trial vanished behind her like a door closing, leaving her in utter blackness.

The raven's wings had carried it out of sight. She had understood then — this would be the trial she faced alone.

The silence pressed against her ears until it rang. She moved forward, though the ground beneath her feet felt more imagined than real. The abyss stretched endless in every direction, yet it wasn't empty — not entirely. Wisps of fog gathered and broke apart, drifting like smoke in water. In some places the fog thickened, curling around itself as though it slithered, alive.

That was when the whispers began.

At first a faint murmur — so soft it might have been her own breath caught in her ears. But then it grew, multiplying, voices overlapping.

"Snow..."
"Snow..."

Her name, breathed from nowhere and everywhere.

Then came panic — the sound of screams tearing through the fog, followed by bursts of laughter, followed by silence. She spun, but no one was there.

The whispers shifted, fragments of conversations unraveling from the shadows. She could not catch the words — broken syllables, murmured prayers, sharp intakes of breath. They tangled together like a thousand voices speaking at once, yet none of them made sense.

The fog thickened before her, writhed and rippled like the coils of a serpent. It slithered across her path, folding over itself, hissing in silence as it shaped itself into faces she thought she recognized — gone again in an instant, dissolving into smoke.

Snow wrapped her arms around herself, though the cold was not of the air but of the whispers sinking beneath her skin. Every step forward was swallowed whole by the abyss, and every breath carried the weight of being watched, studied, mocked.

The whispers grew clearer. Some called her name. Some cried out in terror. Some muttered words she could not decipher.

But all of them came from the fog.

The fog that lived.

The fog slithered at the edge of her vision, thickening into coils, then breaking apart again as if mocking her. Snow's breath came shallow. She had walked through darkness before, had faced illusions of fear and failure, but this was different. This darkness was not absence. It was presence.

The whispers multiplied, climbing over one another until they became a cacophony that pressed against her skull. She could not tell which direction they came from — above, below, inside her. They called her name, they wept, they screamed, they begged.

"Snow…"

"Help me…"

"Why did you leave me?"

Each voice sharper than the last, until she clutched her head to keep them from spilling inside.

And then, woven between the chaos, came a sound that did not belong.

A single tone.

Low. Ancient.

A voice that was not a voice, a language that was not a language.

The whispers bent around it like reeds in wind. At first, Snow thought it was her mind breaking — words she couldn't understand, sounds that clawed into her bones. The dialect had weight, as if each syllable dragged the void closer to swallowing her.

It pulsed through the abyss.

Not Germanic. Not Latin. Not Egyptian. Older. The sound of a tongue spoken before the world had order. A dialect that once consumed all, now curling its syllables between the whispers.

Her breath quickened. She stumbled backward. The fog followed.

The voices screamed louder to hide it, but the deeper tone pressed through, each word carrying venom. She could not understand, yet she knew — in the vibration of her soul — it was speaking to her. Speaking of her.

Snow stood motionless, breath shallow, as the fog thickened into monstrous shapes. At first it seemed only ridges of smoke, but then the black gleam caught her eye—scales vast as ramparts, etched with fractures that burned faintly red, as though volcanic fire still smoldered beneath their surface.

The abyss writhed, and she knew.

This was no formless void. It was a body. A serpent so immense it coiled eternity itself, and she was snared within its endless length.

The ancient voice slithered forth again, deeper now, taking over the marrow within her bones..

"Ahhh…" it hissed, syllables drawn out like the grind of stone. "Your fear perfumes the air. I taste it upon every trembling breath. Your pain—sweet, bitter wine. Your loneliness—ah, it clings to you like ash. You are delicious, child of dust."

The scales shifted closer, scraping the void with their weight. Each surface glistened like polished onyx, cracked with lines of red that pulsed as if blood flowed beneath molten stone.

"You walked willingly into my coil," Apophis rumbled, his dialect now half intelligible, half arcane. "They left you here. Alone. Alone, as you have ever been. Alone, as you shall remain, until I devour what little light you carry."

The abyss quaked with his laughter, not mirthful, but ravenous, the sound of a predator savoring the terror of prey.

Snow's knees weakened. She pressed a hand to her chest, clutching at the Ankh that suddenly felt small, fragile, insignificant in the vastness of his shadow.

The serpent's voice dropped to a whisper, closer now, as if spoken directly against her ear:

"Do you not feel it? No eyes upon you. No hand to hold. No voice to answer. Only me. And I… find you ex*sssssquissssss*ite."

The abyss quivered with a dreadful stillness, then Apophis's voice sank deeper, heavy as a cathedral bell tolling doom.

"You speak of light. You cling to faith. But how does it taste, little pilgrim—knowing you were wrong?"

The words struck like chains.

"Each prayer you whispered, each cry that tore from your throat—it was mine. Your trembling pleas fed me. Each unanswered word fattened the coils that now bind you. Did you never wonder why silence was your only reply? Because your God—" the serpent's laughter crackled like burning timber, "—was never real."

The fog before her convulsed. Shapes tore themselves into being—ragged, fleeting visions:

Her kingdom.

Halls of stone swallowed in fire.

Women screaming. Children running. Men clutching at wounds and crying out for mercy.

Faces twisted in panic, arms outstretched toward Heaven—only to be struck down in silence.

The voices of her people filled the abyss:

"Help us!"

"God, hear us!"

"Why have You forsaken us?"

Snow stumbled backward, clutching her Ankh to her chest as the visions pressed closer, dissolving back into scales.

Apophis's voice rose above the clamor, cruel and vast:

"Did you not see it then? Their prayers, your prayers, none were answered. Not in war, not in famine, not in plague. You called yourself His child, but He left you to wolves and fire. You were never chosen. You were never loved. You were only alone."

The scales groaned around her, tightening, as if the whole abyss sought to crush her beneath its weight.

"Bow to the truth," the serpent whispered, his breath an exhale of ash and stone that turned into a thunderous growl with an ungodly sinister hiss, "You are mine."

The coils of Apophis constricted, the abyss shuddering like a cathedral collapsing in upon itself. Snow staggered, but the serpent's voice did not relent.

"Tell me, daughter of dust—" the syllables slid like molten iron through stone, "did you ever seek to covet what was not yours?"

The fog ignited in ghastly flame, and she beheld her guards raiding foreign lands— torches thrust through windows, screams ringing in the night. Steel flashed, gold was seized, blood painted thresholds. And in the midst of it, a small Snow, no more than a child, watching her aunt's jeweled throne with covetous eyes.

The vision snapped into ash, leaving her trembling.

The serpent's voice swelled darker.

"Did you love your neighbor?"

The abyss wailed. From the fog rose the dead. One by one, then by dozens, then by hundreds—they filled the black like a sea of broken bodies. Men, women, children, peasants and nobles alike. Their eyes clouded, their mouths gaping, their limbs twisted in stillness.

Snow stumbled back, but there was nowhere left to retreat. The corpses pressed against her, pale hands brushing her gown, empty faces turned toward her.

"These were your flock," Apophis hissed. "Each life snuffed beneath your reign. Each death a mark upon your soul. You call yourself chosen, beloved, pure—but see here the truth: you are clothed in blood."

The abyss groaned under the weight of the multitude, the bodies shifting like waves, piling higher, pressing close until the air reeked of rot and smoke.

Snow's chest heaved, tears burning her eyes. The Ankh at her breast felt no heavier than straw, powerless against the tide.

Above her, the serpent's laughter rumbled like thunder through volcanic caverns.

"You prayed for them. You begged for salvation. And yet here they lie—cold, silent, abandoned. Tell me, Snow—was this the hand of your God, or the hand of mine?"

The abyss churned, and the countless corpses did not fade. They lingered, stretching farther than her eye could see — pale faces stacked upon one another, eyeless, still, their silence louder than any scream. Snow's breath broke in ragged gasps as her feet pressed into the dead beneath her.

Apophis's voice thundered from all directions, coiling like fire through stone.

"Look around you, pilgrim. Behold the lives you sent to me. Each soul, each breath, a morsel that swelled my coil. You fed me well with your tyranny."

Snow shook her head, trembling, her arms clutching herself. Her voice, cracked and raw, slipped out unbidden into the abyss.

"No… no, I am not to blame. I did not bring them here… I did not—"

The words had barely left her lips when the air split.

Pain lashed across her back like molten iron, striking with such force it drove her to the ground. She cried out, her palms striking the cold flesh of the dead as she fell among them.

The serpent's laughter curdled into a hiss, heavy with disgust.

"Pathetic." His voice rolled, volcanic and ancient. "So eager to wash your hands in innocence, yet your kingdom drowned in blood. You will not even claim what you wrought."

Another tremor passed through the abyss. The corpses shifted beneath her like waves, their limbs brushing against her arms, their lips parting as if to whisper.

"It is easy," Apophis seethed, his voice pressing close to her ear, "to defend oneself when the victim no longer holds the privilege of breath."

Snow lay among the bodies, her breath shallow, her back seared where the lash had struck. The silence pressed against her, thick, suffocating, until the serpent's voice unfurled once more.

"Ah, how quick you are to cry innocence," Apophis whispered, his tone now sharpened like iron drawn across whetstone. "But tell me—how willing are you to claim it, when those you buried in silence are capable of sharing their truth?"

The abyss trembled.

For a moment all was still. Then a sound pierced the blackness—ragged, wet, a gasp torn from lungs that should not breathe. Snow lifted her head in horror. One of the corpses beside her twitched, its chest heaving, its eyes snapping open clouded and wild.

It screamed.

A sound that split the void—pure panic, a soul ripped back into torment. The figure clawed at the air, stumbling upright, shrieking, "Where am I? What is this place?!"

Snow staggered to her knees, her hands shaking. Another body convulsed. A woman this time, her throat rasping, her eyes wide with terror as she clawed at her own skin. She shrieked into the abyss, "God help me! Where am I?!"

Snow pressed her hands to her ears, but more began to stir.

One by one, the dead writhed to life. Some woke gasping, some thrashing, some already screaming as though aflame. Their cries overlapped until the void thundered with hysteria.

Five bodies. Ten. Fifteen.

The serpent's laughter rumbled through the abyss, deep and dreadful.

Twenty. Twenty-one. Twenty-two.

Snow stumbled back, her heart pounding like a drum in her chest. The dead surged upward around her, their terror filling every corner of the abyss.

Thirty-two. Thirty-three.

Thirty-three voices shrieking, weeping, pleading, clawing at their clothes, their eyes wide with unending panic.

And still, Apophis whispered, curling each syllable like a noose:

"Let them speak, child. Let them tell what your hands have wrought."

The endless screams became one, a single dreadful chorus that rang against the hollow vault of the abyss. Then, as if pulled by some hidden command, their cries faltered. The dead turned.

Every hollow eye, every clouded gaze, fixed upon her.

Snow staggered back, her throat closing, as they reached toward her with shaking hands, voices breaking into words that carved deeper than any blade.

"You promised…"

"You swore we would be safe."

"Why, Snow? Why did you abandon us?"

Their mouths, slack with terror moments before, now trembled with accusation.

And the wounds they bore — oh God, the wounds.

From the dwarf village came charred forms, their flesh blackened and crumbling, their hair burnt to ash. Smoke still curled from their mouths as they moaned her name.

The huntsman rose, his headless body staggering forward. Beside him, his wife and daughter clutched their bellies, torsos still split and gaping, entrails hanging like rotten garlands — never stitched, never honored. Their hollow eyes dripped with despair as they whispered, *"Why did you leave us so?"*

Behind them, the soldiers she once led dragged themselves upright. Some bore spears driven clear through their bodies, others hacked in half, still reaching with broken arms toward their queen.

And then—faces she knew by heart.

Her childhood friends, their laughter now twisted into sobs, blood matting their hair. The market folk, their aprons burned, their baskets overturned, their hands blackened with soot and steel.

More and more surged from the sea of corpses — men, women, children, loyal subjects by the hundreds. Each face carved with its final suffering. Each mouth opened with one word:

"Why?"

The multitude pressed in. Hands clawed at her gown, tore at her arms, shoved her backward into the tide of the dead. Fingers scraped her skin, nails dragging across her flesh, as their wails rose to a frenzy.

Snow screamed, twisting, shoving, but they engulfed her, their hands unrelenting, their eyes burning with accusation. The weight of their bodies, the stink of their wounds, the despair of their voices — all of it closed in, drowning her in a sea of broken promises.

And above it all, Apophis laughed, the sound shaking the abyss like the cracking of stone.

Snow thrashed against the press of bodies, their touch no longer mere clawing but a dreadful theft. Rotten hands dug into her flesh, tearing at her sleeves, scraping her skin as if to rip strips from her living body. Their fingers pressed deeper, clutching at her arms, her neck, her thighs, as though her unbroken skin might serve as patches to cover their own gaping wounds.

The stench of decay filled her lungs. Her screams broke ragged, swallowed by the swarm. Her nails clawed at the hands, but still they clung, their whispers rising into howls of desperation.

"Give us back what you stole."

"Share your flesh with ours."

"You owe us!"

Her vision blurred, her head falling back, the weight of the multitude pressing her down into the sea of the dead. Her eyelids fluttered as darkness pulled at her.

Then—silence.

Snow gasped and forced her eyes open.

The corpses were gone. The stench had vanished. The abyss yawned empty once more, stretching endless and still.

And then, from the hollow void, came a voice. Soft. Familiar. Piercing through the silence with a single word:

"Mother?" Snow whispered, her breath breaking on the word.

Her voice echoed into the emptiness, trembling, fragile.

Snow's breath rattled as her whisper faded into the abyss. The silence stretched, then trembled, and the fog began to stir. The coils shifted, vast and terrible, their ridges etched in volcanic fire.

And within them, through the murk, a figure emerged.

Her mother.

Pale, wandering, her hands clutching at the dark as though blind, her gown in tatters. Her voice cracked as she cried into the abyss:

"Where are you? My family... where are you?!"

Snow's throat closed. She reached forward a trembling hand, but the fog pressed between them, thick as iron bars.

Her mother stumbled, arms outstretched, her hair matted with sweat and ash. Her voice rose higher, breaking into sobs.

"God, why am I alone? Why did You leave me here? Why do You not answer?"

Her voice echoed across the coils, desperate, pleading.

"Is this what comes after? Endless torment? Silence?!"

Snow shook her head, her tears spilling hot down her cheeks. "No—no, Mother…" she whispered, but her voice drowned in the dark.

Her mother fell to her knees, clawing at the unseen ground, her sobs shattering into screams.

"Answer me! Please—why will You not answer me?!"

The coils shivered, the serpent's laughter rumbling beneath the cries. The fog around her mother darkened, swallowing her light.

And then, with a voice broken by anguish, Snow's mother raised her face to the abyss and cried:

"Then I forsake You!"

Her scream tore through the dark, raw with fury and despair, before the fog consumed her form, snuffing her like a dying flame.

Snow's heart broke within her chest, her own voice tearing free as she screamed into the void, "No! Mother, no!"

But only silence answered her.

The coils rumbled with a laughter that shook the abyss.

"Ahhh," Apophis hissed, the words curling like venom.

"There… your mother learned the truth. She begged. She pleaded. She wailed into silence until her heart cracked and her tongue spat out the lie she once cherished. She learned she was wrong. Just as you are wrong."

The fog quivered, then opened again. Another vision took form—broad shoulders, regal robes now torn and blackened by soot.

Her father.

He stood upon a field of ruin. Behind him, the smoldering wreckage of a village— timbers split, homes reduced to ash, the cries of women and children drowned in silence. Before him, the battlefield stretched—a ghastly sea of severed limbs, spears thrust through corpses, and blood-soaked mud.

He looked upon it all with eyes hollow, his crown heavy upon his brow.

At first he stood tall, as sovereign king. But then his shoulders sagged. His knees trembled, buckled, and he fell.

Snow gasped as his palms struck the earth, his body wracked with sobs. Tears streamed down his face as he lifted his eyes to the heavens.

"This—this is the God I served?" he choked, his voice raw. "This silence, this cruelty, this endless grief?!"

His arms thrust upward, trembling hands clawing at the unseen firmament above.

"I forsake You!" he roared, his voice breaking into fury. "I was told to honor and respect You! I was told to cherish Your name! But You are a liar, a falsehood, a grave-digger of nations! I forsake You!"

The battlefield quaked beneath him, corpses shifting, fires rising as if to swallow the vision whole.

Apophis's laughter thundered again, rattling through the coils.

"Your father… your sovereign… even he, child, saw the truth. He saw that all his prayers, all his honor, all his faith was but a banquet for me. And so he spat upon your God and cast Him aside."

The coils pressed tighter, the volcanic scales glowing faintly as though a furnace burned just beneath.

The abyss quaked with the serpent's mirth, his laughter searing through the dark like fire spilling from broken stone.

"They turned, your mother and father. They saw truth where you still clutch at lies. And yet… still you do not understand."

The coils shifted, scales scraping like grinding boulders. The fog thickened, then parted once more.

From its depths stepped two figures.

Her parents.

Not as she remembered them—noble, dignified—but wan and cold, their faces carved in sorrow. Their eyes, pale and empty, fixed upon her with a weight she could not bear.

"Tell me, Snow," Apophis hissed, his voice curdling into mock solemnity. "Did you honor your mother and father?"

Snow's lips trembled, her breath shaking as her parents' forms drifted nearer, pale spectres lit by the glow of volcanic scales.

Her mother's voice was soft, breaking like glass:

"If only we had lived another life… if only we had listened to your aunt…"

Her father's jaw clenched, his hands trembling at his sides. His eyes brimmed not with love but with an unbearable disappointment.

"We wasted ourselves on you," he rasped. "All our hope, all our pride… and look at what you have wrought. A kingdom in ruin. A child unworthy."

The two of them stood side by side in the serpent's abyss, their shoulders heavy with regret.

"If only," her mother whispered again, tears sliding down her cheeks, "if only we had never wasted our time on you."

Snow staggered, her body quaking. "No… no, that's not true… Mother, Father—"

But the abyss devoured her voice, leaving only the sound of her parents' sorrow, echoing louder, sharper, until it drowned even her own heart.

Snow's voice cracked as she tried to speak, but her father's roar split the abyss and silenced her.

"Enough!"

The word struck like a hammer on iron. His face twisted, his tears now burning with rage.

"I gave you everything," he thundered, his voice shaking the fog, shaking her to her knees. "Every chance to make this kingdom strong, to honor our house, to leave behind a legacy

78

of greatness. I gave you men who would bleed for you—loyal followers who loved this family more than their own lives!"

His hand trembled as he pointed at her, his arm rigid as steel.

"And you shut your doors to them. You turned their devotion into ash. You killed our legacy with your cowardice. You may as well have been the blade that struck me down yourself!"

His chest heaved, his body trembling with fury, yet his eyes—those eyes she once sought comfort in—glowed with nothing but loathing.

Beside him, her mother said nothing.

She only stared at Snow with a face carved from stone. Her eyes were cold, stranger's eyes, as if the girl before her bore no blood of hers at all. There was no love in them, no softness—only disdain.

As her father's tirade echoed into the endless coils, her mother's gaze pressed deeper, hollow with judgment.

Her silence said more than words ever could: *You disrespected my husband. You ripped away the future I bore for you. And now you dare stand before me, seeking validation?*

The weight of her stare smothered Snow, until she could not breathe.

Apophis's laughter rippled low through the abyss, savoring every fracture in her soul.

Snow's father's voice faded into a rumble, his fury dissolving into the coils. Only her mother remained, stepping forward with quiet, dreadful poise. Her eyes never left Snow's face.

When she spoke, her voice was low, ragged, but sharp as a blade:

"All I see, when I look upon you… is my death."

Snow's breath caught.

"That is all you gave me to remember. Your face—hovering above me in my coffin-as if you weren't the reason I rotted away in its frame. Your face—etched upon the ruin of my body. My death is all you left me. And now… I give it back to you."

Her mother's hand, pale and trembling, rose and pressed against Snow's cheek.

Agony ignited.

Snow screamed—or tried to, but her throat seized. Fire raced beneath her skin, ripping outward as though her flesh could no longer contain it. Her organs twisted, pulling against their moorings, clawing to escape. Her chest burned with the weight of poison, of unfulfilled dreams curdling into ash.

She clawed at her own body, her nails tearing against her gown as if to tear the pain free, but it would not release her. Her lungs seized; no breath would come. Her voice broke into silence, her mouth gaping wide as she drowned in agony that was not hers, yet was forced into her as her inheritance.

She fell to the ground, writhing, her eyes rolling as the world spun. Panic seized her heart. She could not breathe. She could not scream. She was trapped in her mother's death.

And all the while, the fog shifted.

The coils of Apophis stirred around her, vast and patient, circling like a predator savoring the kill. Black scales glistened with volcanic fire as they wound nearer, sliding over one another in dreadful silence.

Snow's chest convulsed. At last, air tore into her lungs like broken glass. She gasped, choking, her body shaking as she clung to the breath she thought forever lost.

And then the coils closed.

Black scales, vast and gleaming with molten fissures, wound tight around her body. Her feet left the ground as Apophis's terrible strength pulled her upright, his grip a prison of stone and fire.

She writhed, but each movement drew the coils tighter. Her ribs groaned, her shoulders strained, yet she could still draw shallow breaths, each one sharp with terror.

The air grew hotter. Then she felt it.

A sickening tingle brushed her ear—the forked tongue of the serpent, writhing like living flame. Her skin crawled as it traced the edge of her neck, and then the voice came—hissing, ancient, dreadful.

Not in words she knew, but in the tongue that had consumed the world before order was carved from chaos. Each syllable slithered into her mind like venom, heavy with unease, their meaning unknown but their malice clear.

Snow's body stiffened, her eyes wide with horror. She dared not move, for every flinch, every tremor, drew the coils tighter still.

She breathed, but she did not know for how long.

The abyss rumbled with the serpent's language, each sound pressing deeper into her soul.

The coils held her fast, her body rigid against their crushing weight. The serpent's voice writhed through her skull, the ancient syllables burning like brands upon her soul. She clenched her jaw, fighting to block them out, but there was no escape.

Then, slowly, the words sharpened, slipping into her understanding like a dagger through cloth.

"Do you not see, child?" Apophis hissed, his tone dripping with cruel delight. "There is nothing left for you. Your prayers are ash. Your family, faithless. Your kingdom, dust. There is only me. Chaos. I am what remains. You are not alone, for I am with you."

The coils constricted, and the abyss shivered at his proclamation.

Snow's breath caught, her chest heaving against the crushing grip. For a moment her heart stilled beneath the weight of those words, as though he had spoken her reckoning into being.

And then—

A cry.

Faint, quivering, filled with fear.

"Help... someone... please..."

Snow's eyes widened. It was no illusion of fire or battle, no vision of parent or corpse. It was the voice of innocence, breaking against the walls of chaos.

Dopey.

Another cry, sharper now, desperate.

"Where am I? I don't understand—"

The sound tore through the abyss, pure terror, pure confusion.

And Snow's blood turned to ice.

The cry lingered in the abyss, fragile, trembling, innocent. Snow's breath caught in her throat, her eyes burning with tears that refused to fall.

And then it came.

A sound not of body, but of psyche. The sharp, crystalline fracture of something breaking deep within her, echoing like a shattered bell.

Her soul.

The coils quivered as if savoring it.

Apophis hissed with delight, his tongue writhing against her ear.

"Ahhh…," he hissed, "there it is. The sweet shatter. I taste it… your despair, your breaking. Each crack feeds me. Each fragment, a draught of wine."

Snow trembled, her body limp within his coils, her spirit quaking.

Dopey's voice returned—shaking, stumbling, words tumbling out in panic.

"I—I don't know where I am… what's happening? Please… someone… I'm scared… so scared…"

His voice cracked, splintering, until it rose in a single, gut-wrenching scream that tore through the abyss.

It pierced her heart, raw and ragged, a child's cry that no darkness should ever hold.

And then silence.

The echo of Dopey's scream had scarcely faded when Apophis's laughter slithered through the coils, dark and ravenous.

"Such innocence," he mocked, his voice curling with lustful delight. "Such fragile sweetness, breaking like glass. He is yours, is he not? Your child of light, your fool of joy—and now mine to feast upon. Listen well, Snow, and drink of his despair."

Dopey's voice broke again—pleading now, weak and stumbling.

"Please—stop... I'll be good... I just want to go home..."

Then another cry, shorter, strangled—drowned beneath the sudden roar of laughter. Demonic mirth rose on all sides, jeering, shrieking with glee. It swelled until it shook the abyss itself, a chorus of cruelty that cheered with every broken sound that left Dopey's lips.

"Louder!" Apophis hissed. "Do you hear them? They rejoice in his torment! They exalt in his pain! This is the banquet you left him to, child of dust!"

The cries and laughter tangled together, growing, swelling, until the darkness itself seemed to chant with joy.

Dopey's voice faltered, weakening, each plea quieter than the last. Still present, but fading.

Snow screamed, thrashing in the coils, her body convulsing as her hands clawed toward her face. Her nails scraped across her skin as she pressed hard against her ears, desperate to drown it out, to silence the torment that threatened to shatter her mind.

The sound of her soul splitting came again—louder, sharper, like iron snapping under unbearable weight.

Her chest heaved. Her eyes rolled. Her spirit quivered at the brink, ready to burst.

And still the laughter raged.

Snow's screams broke raw in her throat, her body convulsing as she pressed her hands to her ears. The cacophony tore at her—Dopey's pleading cries fading, the demons' laughter rising, Apophis's venom slithering deeper.

Her chest ached as if splintering from within. Her breath came in jagged sobs, salt tears blinding her eyes. The coils pressed tighter, grinding her bones, every tremor of her body stoking the serpent's delight.

"Break," he whispered, his tongue flicking against her skin. "Break, and be mine."

Snow gasped, choking, her sobs collapsing into silence. Her arms trembled, her hands pulling at her hair, clawing, desperate to tear herself free from the voices that would not cease.

And then—she felt it.

Something small. Something out of place.

Through her tangled hair, her shaking fingers brushed against it—soft, smooth, yet firm.

She pulled it free, her breath shuddering, her eyes swimming with tears.

A feather.

Black as the void. Its edge glinted faintly in the molten glow of the serpent's coils.

The raven.

Snow's chest heaved. Her throat ached. She stared through tear-soaked eyes at the fragile token in her hand.

And in that moment of agony, both body and soul wracked to breaking, she whispered, half-laughing, half-sobbing:

"You never left."

The words slipped weakly from her lips, yet they fell heavier than all the serpent's venom.

Snow's hand shook as she clutched the feather, her tears spilling over it until the dark shaft gleamed wet in the dim glow. Her breath rattled, her ribs crushed within the coils, yet she held it close as though it were life itself.

Relief broke over her—not release from pain, but a recognition. This was no abandonment. The raven had flown ahead, but it had not forsaken her.

The feather was proof.

Her sobs quieted into trembling breaths. Through the blur of her tears, she saw not only the blackness that surrounded her, but beyond it. Beyond the coils. Beyond the screams. Beyond the torment.

There is something more… something greater than this abyss. A place of beauty, of light, of rest.

Her soul whispered to itself: *Perhaps not for me. This is my path. This is my atonement. But this torment is not Dopey's story. His innocence is not meant to die here.*

Snow's heart, though wracked with agony, held fast to that truth.

She pressed the feather to her lips and closed her eyes.

The coils convulsed in rage. Apophis's laughter turned to a roar that cracked through the abyss like volcanic thunder.

"You dare defy me with hope?" he seethed. "You dare cling to light when I have devoured worlds?"

His body constricted, black scales grinding over one another, volcanic fissures glowing red. Snow's ribs cracked under the pressure, splintering sharp within her chest. Her collar bone snapped like a dry twig in winter's grip. Her pelvis groaned, hips rolling, bones grinding against themselves as though crushed to powder.

Snow's vision blurred white with agony. Each breath was a battle, every gasp shredded in her throat.

With the feather still clutched in her trembling hand, she forced air through her lips, whispering through tears, through blood:

"Save him, please… He is innocent… deserving of eternal peace and love… Leave me… take me… but spare him, please…"

Her voice broke into choking. Her body seized, her limbs numbing beneath the serpent's crushing hold.

The coils crushed tighter, the last breath trembling upon Snow's lips—when the abyss shuddered.

A burst of light tore open the black, flooding the void in brilliance so pure it seared the eyes. The laughter of demons was silenced in an instant, swallowed by radiance.

Before Snow's failing vision, a path unfolded. It stretched out across the abyss like glass forged from heaven itself, pristine and clear, as though she might walk upon air. Each shard caught the glow, refracting it into a thousand glimmers, a bridge carved of light where there had been only void.

And upon that path—she came.

Tawaret.

Her form was terrible and beautiful all at once. A woman of full and powerful figure, her body draped in fine white linen that shimmered like starlight. Heavy jewels gleamed upon her throat and wrists, sapphires and emeralds woven into gold, each piece glinting with sacred power.

Yet her head bore the shape of the hippopotamus, fierce and majestic, tusks curved, eyes gleaming with eternal fire. Her presence radiated motherhood, fierce as a lioness yet tender as a cradle. She was sacrifice, protection, endurance given form.

The coils of Apophis recoiled, shuddering beneath the brilliance, his hiss drowned in the rising hum of light.

Snow, broken and trembling, beheld her through tears.

And for the first time in the abyss, she felt the weight of love, not as frailty, but as shield.

The serpent's coils recoiled with a hiss, and Snow's broken body fell, cast down onto the glass path. She struck hard, her frame shuddering against its radiant surface. For a moment she lay still, trembling, her breath ragged, her limbs heavy as stone.

Broken—yet not defeated.

Light swelled above her. Tawaret stepped forward, her white linen shimmering in the abyss, her jeweled form radiant with fierce compassion. She knelt, towering yet tender, and laid her massive hand upon the Ankh that hung against Snow's breast.

At her touch, the symbol ignited. Lotus light burst forth, flooding its hollow with blossoms of white fire.

Snow gasped, her eyes widening as warmth surged through her body. The broken bones knit together with a deep, resonant ache. Her skin, torn and bruised, closed with fresh strength. The ragged silence of her throat was healed, vocal cords threading themselves whole once more.

Tawaret's hand remained steady, lifting her gently. Snow rose from the path, her body mended by light, her spirit steadied by the strength of the goddess.

She stood—not untouched, but restored.

Snow's body trembled as the lotus light surged through her, mending what had been broken. She stood upon the glass path, the raven's feather still clutched in her hand, her chest heaving with the memory of torment.

Tawaret's gaze, motherly and fierce, settled upon her. When she spoke, her voice rolled through the abyss like the hymn of creation itself—low, steady, unshaken.

"You did not yield."

Her tusked mouth softened into something near a smile, her jeweled form gleaming brighter with every word.

"You were crushed, torn, burned, broken—but you did not forsake the light. Even when despair offered you an easier path, you clung to love. You offered your life, your eternity, that another might be spared. That child's innocence you counted greater than your own salvation."

Snow's eyes burned with tears, her lips trembling, though no words rose from her throat.

Tawaret leaned closer, her voice thick with both sorrow and pride.

"This is the only power Chaos cannot consume: faith. Love. The giving of oneself for another. Eternal damnation for salvation. You offered yourself to the void so another might taste peace. In this, you triumphed. And in this, you wounded him."

The coils of Apophis hissed in the distance, unseen but restless, his fury trembling through the abyss at her words.

Tawaret's hand remained steady upon Snow's shoulder.

"The serpent will rage. He will twist. He will tear. But he cannot conquer faith, and he cannot devour love."

Tawaret's hand fell from Snow's shoulder, the glow of the lotus fading gently into the Ankh. The goddess straightened, her linen robes whispering against the glass path, her jewels catching the shimmer of light.

She turned and began to walk, her great figure steady and sure, the path gleaming beneath her feet. Snow, still trembling but restored, followed in silence.

As they walked, Tawaret's voice rose again, firm yet tender:

"You are no longer the girl you once were. But neither are you yet the woman you must become. This Pilgrimage is shaping you, stripping you, breaking and remaking you. Where you go now, you shall be weighed—not by words or illusions, but by the truth of your heart."

The light of the glass path began to dim as they approached the end. There, carved into the abyss itself, stood a stairway of stone.

Its steps descended into shadow, their edges rough and ancient. Torches lined the walls, their flames sputtering with eerie green light. Gargoyles crouched at intervals, their wings unfurled, their stone mouths frozen in snarls as though guarding what lay below.

Tawaret halted at the stair's edge. She turned to Snow once more, her gaze solemn, her tusked face illuminated by the unnatural flame.

"It is time," she said. "The Chamber of the Scales awaits you. I can go no further."

Snow's hand clutched the raven's feather. The lotus light pulsed softly within her Ankh.

The abyss behind her lay silent. The stairway before her beckoned.

And with Tawaret's final nod, Snow stepped forward to descend.

Trial 5: Unspoken Truths

"Then you will know the truth, and the truth will set you free."

John 8:32

Snow set her foot upon the first step, and the stone shuddered beneath her weight as though the stairway itself remembered every soul that had ever dared to walk it. From the abyss below, a wail rose — not one voice, but a thousand unsettled souls, screaming in endless anguish. Their cries clawed at the walls, shrill and hollow, while from deeper still came the guttural roar of unseen beasts, their hunger palpable, their excitement swelling at the scent of new prey.

Her chest tightened, breath catching as she looked into the vast dark pressing against the stair. For a heartbeat she feared the shadows themselves would surge forward and tear her down into the pit.

But then — the fire held. The ancient torches, rooted in the very stone, flared as though awakened by her steps. Their flames hissed and spat, but not in weakness — each one burned with a power older than time, pushing back the black tide. The darkness recoiled, kept at bay by the sacred fire.

The stairway was no crafted marvel of men, no careful work of chisels or rails. It was hewn from the core of the earth itself, jagged and eternal, a descent into judgment that could never be remade or erased.

Snow drew in a trembling breath. The way forward was terrible, but it was also protected — a path carved before the first stone temple, meant only for those who dared to face what awaited below.

Snow pressed onward, one step, then another. With each descent her pulse steadied, the terror of the shrieking souls and ravenous beasts giving way to a fragile, unspoken calm. She knew this hush was no mercy — it was the calm before the next trial, the breath the world takes before it breaks.

Her eyes lifted to the shadows that lined the stair. For so long she had thought them gargoyles, twisted stone guardians leering in silence. Yet as the dust shifted with her passing, the illusion faltered. What had seemed corroded and grotesque sharpened, gleamed, transformed.

It was a trick of the dust — a test of her resolve, meant to weigh her fear against her faith. She had not turned back. She had not cowered. And so the path rewarded her with clarity.

What she now beheld were not gargoyles at all, but statues of flawless gold. Their surfaces blazed in the torchlight, every detail rendered in perfect majesty.

The first figures rose out of the haze, towering and resplendent in their gilded glory.

Set stood in eternal defiance, his entire form — from the sweep of his jackal-like head to the breadth of his shoulders — cast in flawless gold. His helm and armor gleamed as though hammered by storms themselves, each plate etched with patterns of fire, desert winds, and cruel precision. The angles of his golden face, sharp and unyielding, held the same terrible majesty as when Snow had faced him in flesh. Even rendered in statue, he remained intimidating, a presence that pressed against her chest like a weight of iron.

Beside him loomed the Sha, the beast no world could name, its elongated snout and squared ears sculpted into unnatural permanence. Though frozen in gold, its form still unsettled her, the memory of its otherness stirring unease.

The firelight danced over them, igniting their surfaces as though the gods still pulsed beneath the metal. Snow slowed, her breath catching in recognition. The memory of Set's illusions returned — that endless walk through her failures, every step meant to unravel her. She remembered how the despair had nearly undone her… and how, in surviving it, she had uncovered a resilience she had not known remained.

Her eyes lingered on the Sha, its posture poised as if mocking her with silence. But she did not flinch. She bore its shadow still, not as an open wound, but as a scar — proof that she had strength enough to deny temptation's thirst.

Snow descended another step. Set and his beast watched, silent and golden, and though their presence remained as oppressive as ever, she felt a quiet strength rise within her.

The torchlight trembled, and the next figures emerged from the haze.

Bastet stood radiant, her cat's head sculpted in flawless gold, ears rising sharp and regal like a crown. Her eyes, though blind in metal, seemed to glimmer with the promise of both fury and tenderness. Her body was carved in pristine form — strong, supple, the perfect union of grace and might. She was elegance made eternal, her golden poise a silent hymn to protection and wrath alike.

Beside her towered Khonshu, every fold of his robed body chiseled in gleaming gold, yet crowned with the terrible beauty of a falcon's skull, also transfigured into radiant metal. Its empty sockets stared forward with immortal severity, as if death and time themselves had been gilded and set in place for judgment. He seemed less a statue than a celestial pillar, the eternal witness of the moon's unyielding gaze.

Beside them arched the sinuous body of the Serpopard. Its long, coiling neck and leonine haunches were shaped from gold that rippled like liquid fire. Muscles caught in divine tension bulged beneath scales that shimmered in the torchlight. Its teeth, sharp and eternal, seemed to glint as though ready to tear through stone. Though still, the air around it vibrated with the memory of its primal roar.

Together the three blazed like an unbreakable triad — the cat, the falcon, and the beast. Snow's breath caught in her chest. In their presence she felt the echo of what they had

taught her: the necessity of joy even in despair, the guidance of the moon when paths were shrouded, and the courage to face the beast within and without.

The stair bent lower, and the torches flared again. From the veil of dust, two more figures emerged in blazing majesty.

Sekhmet towered in full golden form, her lioness head lifted high, fangs bared in a snarl that even eternity could not tame. Her mane flowed like fire hammered into metal, strands etched with impossible precision, each one a flame frozen in gold. Her body radiated divine strength — shoulders broad, arms sculpted to strike with irresistible might, every line a testament to war and wrath. Yet within her poise there was no chaos, only a fierce balance — the predator held in perfect command.

Beside her stretched Aker, the twin lion-bodies fused back to back, carved into an endless golden arch. Their forms mirrored in flawless symmetry, one gazing forward, the other behind, guardians of past and future. The gold caught the firelight and seemed to shift with it, bending like a horizon at dawn and dusk. Time itself seemed captured in their eternal watch, the threshold between what was and what would come.

Snow slowed as she passed, awe pressing down upon her. In their gaze, she remembered what Sekhmet had demanded of her — the courage to embrace both destruction and protection, the fire to burn away fear. And in Aker's arch she recalled how the path had stretched between past sorrow

and future despair, and how she had been forced to walk as both protector and witness.

The stairway plunged deeper, and the next torch hissed, spilling its light across two more radiant figures.

Tawaret rose first with her golden hippopotamus head. Her body, though heavy and towering, was carved in divine poise — thick limbs and rounded form shaped not in clumsiness but in fierce protection. In gold she was both mother and sentinel, the eternal guardian of birth, rebirth, and the fragile flame of life. Her presence pressed against Snow like an embrace of iron — unyielding, immovable, a promise that no darkness could shatter what she shielded.

Across from her coiled Apophis, the great serpent of chaos. His endless body was etched in molten arcs of gold, every scale catching the torchlight like shards of shattered suns. His jaws gaped wide, fangs hooked and venomous, frozen forever in the act of swallowing creation. Even carved in stillness, his form seemed to writhe, the illusion of motion slithering over the gilded surface. His presence was terror itself, bound into metal yet threatening to break free at any moment.

Snow felt the weight of them both — protector and devourer, nurture and annihilation — the twin forces that had shaped her last trial. In Tawaret she remembered the sacrifice she had embraced, faith stronger than death. In Apophis she recalled the abyss she had faced, and the victory of love that had cast it back.

The stair dipped lower, and the firelight unveiled the next guardians.

Anubis towered above the steps, wrought entirely of gold. His jackal head gleamed in flawless precision, long ears reaching upward like spears of judgment, muzzle sharpened into eternal severity. His body was carved in commanding stillness — broad chest, arms folded across him, as though even in statue he presided over all truth and falsehood. He was unreadable, his gaze fixed forward, impartial and eternal. Nothing in his form betrayed mercy, nor malice — only judgment, carved into gold.

Yet at his feet coiled the Demonic Gatekeepers. Unlike the statues she had passed before, these were no serene witnesses. Their bodies were twisted in feral crouches, claws hooked, jaws parted in silent hunger. Their golden faces were carved in grotesque sneers, fangs bared, eyes narrowed in ravenous delight. And though they were bound in metal, Snow felt their eagerness — the thrill of predators waiting to be loosed.

She halted, standing in their presence. Her breath slowed, her chest tight. The torchlight shimmered across Anubis' still, unyielding frame... and over the Gatekeepers' snarling hunger.

A thought pressed hard into her mind, as undeniable as the stone beneath her feet:

This was her next trial.

Snow pressed forward, the weight of Anubis' gaze still pressing at her back. As her foot fell past his towering form, the silence broke.

The Demonic Gatekeepers stirred. Their golden claws scraped softly against the stone, shoulders rolling as if shaking off centuries of stillness. Their mouths curled wider, lips pulling back over jagged teeth. Slowly, they slipped from their crouches, shadows flickering across their gilded frames as they began to move.

They followed. Silent, stalking, their hunger cloaked in patience. Snow did not turn; she did not see. The stairway shielded her in ignorance, her eyes fixed forward. But the Gatekeepers lingered at her heels, their presence slithering closer with every step.

The next torch flared, revealing Ma'at in her perfect poise. Her golden wings stretched outward, feather upon feather etched in radiant symmetry, each one catching the fire as though aflame with truth. Her eyes, carved in divine serenity, gazed forward in calm judgment. Beside her crouched Ammit, the Devourer, her body a seamless union of lion, crocodile, and hippopotamus — each monstrous form cast into flawless gold. Her jaws gaped wide, frozen forever in the act of consuming, the very embodiment of punishment for unworthy souls.

Snow's steps slowed, her chest heavy. Truth and annihilation — side by side, eternal. She felt their weight press upon her, not as choice but as certainty.

She moved again. The next fire hissed, and the final figures emerged.

Thoth, ibis-headed, stood tall with his scroll pressed to his chest, his golden feathers etched with such precision they seemed ready to stir in a phantom wind. His beak curved sharp and knowing, his eyes narrowed in wisdom eternal. At his side crouched the Sphinx, its leonine body rippling with sculpted power, human face flawless and unreadable, lips curved in the faintest hint of a riddle left unspoken. Together they radiated the inevitability of record and question — the one who would inscribe her truth, and the one who would demand she understand it.

Snow descended past them, the stairway opening into the chamber floor below. The torches crackled above her, the golden gods and beasts standing sentinel in their eternal ranks. Yet in the shadows behind her, the Gatekeepers crept, eager and waiting for the moment to bare their teeth.

Snow stepped off the final stair, her foot touching the chamber floor. The air changed.

The hall stretched wide before her, cavernous yet precise, its vastness bound by an invisible order. The walls curved and intersected with such perfection that her skin prickled. It was not emptiness she entered, but a design older than temples, a pattern carved from eternity itself. Each angle and line sang in harmony with the others, sacred geometry woven into stone, and with every step she took into the center, her body vibrated with its resonance.

Her breath caught. The trembling of her heart steadied into rhythm with the chamber's pulse. For a moment, she closed her eyes, allowing it to wash through her — the energy of balance, of divine measure, filling her bones with something she could not name.

Then she opened them.

There, in the chamber's heart, stood the Scales — vast, monumental, their beam stretching twice as tall as she. The metal gleamed in the firelight, heavy and waiting, ancient beyond imagining.

Behind them loomed Anubis, no longer statue but towering in solemn stillness, his jackal head unreadable, his presence pressing down like the weight of the earth itself.

And perched atop the Scales was the Raven. Its feathers glistened dark as oil, each movement catching the fire in fleeting sheen. Black eyes glared down, unblinking, as though it had been waiting for her all along.

Unseen, in the edges of the shadows, the Gatekeepers crept, circling, their hunger hidden, their patience sharpening with every step she took toward judgment.

Snow stood motionless at the center, her breath shallow, her chest rising and falling in careful rhythm. The chamber seemed to hum around her, every stone vibrating with a power she could neither command nor resist. The Scales gleamed before her, vast and unyielding, while Anubis loomed in silence, a figure of impenetrable judgment. The Raven shifted upon the beam, feathers whispering as wings folded close again, its black eyes piercing her as though it had been waiting for this very moment.

For a heartbeat, she felt small. Not broken, not diminished, but a single fragile flame caught in the vast design of eternity. Awe rooted her where she stood, and though dread weighed her heart, she did not turn away.

The silence cracked.

From the shadows, the Gatekeepers stirred, their golden forms slipping free of the dark. They circled wide around her, claws scraping softly, eyes gleaming with anticipation. When they spoke, their voices rasped like stone across stone, ancient and cold.

"Behold the Judge," one intoned, gesturing toward the jackal god who stood in towering stillness.

"He is the Keeper of the Scales," hissed another, its words drawn out, as though savoring the weight.

"He will not speak for you," said a third. "He will not bend, nor yield. He is silence — and in silence, truth is revealed."

Their circle tightened, slow and deliberate.

"You have not come here for mercy," the Gatekeepers whispered together, their voices overlapping like the hiss of a thousand serpents. "You have come to speak what you have hidden. To bare what rots in shadow. Only then will the Scales awaken."

Snow's throat tightened. Her eyes lifted again to the towering form of Anubis — silent, unreadable, eternal. The Gatekeepers' words rang through her, echoing against the walls of her own heart.

The Gatekeepers' words faded, leaving only the hum of the chamber and the crushing silence of Anubis' stare. Snow's breath rattled in her chest, her hands trembling at her sides. For a moment she closed her eyes, and in the dark behind her lids the truth burned, rising clearer than it ever had before.

Her Pilgrimage had stripped her bare. Every illusion, every trial had cut deeper, peeling away the defenses she once hid behind. Now there was nothing left but the truth she had carried like a stone in her chest.

Snow lifted her gaze to the jackal god towering above the Scales. She felt small, infinitesimal beneath his shadow, and yet she could not keep silent. Her voice shook as it left her lips.

"I blamed *Him*," she whispered. The words caught in her throat, jagged and sharp, but they spilled out nonetheless. "I blamed God for all of it — for the ruin, for the treachery, for the betrayals that hollowed my life. I blamed Him for the cruelty that stalked my every step."

Her eyes brimmed, but her voice hardened.

"Worse than blame…" She drew a trembling breath. "I hated Him."

The chamber seemed to still, the torches hissing softly in the silence.

"I hated Him for taking my mother. For taking my father. For locking me in a coffin, a bird with its wings cut, left to wither in a glass cage — admired, yes, but never free. I hated that He made me weak, fragile, in need of constant saving." Her voice dropped lower, thick with grief.

Her hands balled into fists at her sides.

"But most of all," she breathed, her voice breaking, "I hated Him for what He gave me. For the loves I held so fiercely, so desperately, only to have them torn from me again and again. He gave me everything I could not bear to lose… and then ripped it away."

The words echoed into the vast chamber, reverberating through the sacred geometry until they felt etched into the very stone.

No answer came from Anubis. His silence bore down heavier than stone. But the stillness did not last.

The Gatekeepers moved. They slunk from the edges of shadow into the circle of torchlight, their golden claws dragging against the floor in slow arcs. They circled her like carrion, their mouths twisting into sneers that shimmered in the firelight.

"Half the truth…" one rasped, its voice low and curling like smoke.

"Half only," another hissed, pacing behind her shoulder.

"You cannot hide from it," the third growled. "Not here. Not before him."

They drew closer, the rhythm of their voices tightening like a snare.

"Speak it. Speak it. SPEAK it."

The chorus pressed into her ears, into her chest, until her breath broke. Tears flooded Snow's eyes, falling hot across her cheeks. She looked down, unable to hold their gaze, her lids shutting tight as though darkness could shield her.

Her palms opened in a trembling gesture of surrender, rising weakly at her sides. She motioned helplessly, wordless — as if to say she did not know how to shape the torment into sound, as if she begged for the words to be torn from her without her having to speak them.

Still the voices pressed closer.

"Speak it. Speak it. Speak it…"

The chamber throbbed with their demand.

Snow's hands shook as she held them open, trembling in her own helplessness. The Gatekeepers circled, voices grinding against her like chains. Her tears streamed faster, falling to the stone below, when—

Warmth.

A hand enclosed hers, steady and calm. Then another, firm but gentle, wrapping around her trembling fingers. The voices dulled at once, their edge blunted. Snow froze, her breath catching in her throat. She knew these hands before she even opened her eyes.

She let the final tears fall, sliding down her face as she slowly lifted her gaze.

It was Doc.

He stood before her, small in stature but unshaken, his grip sure and unyielding against her faltering strength. His eyes met hers, steady and clear, carrying the weight of all the years he had stood by her side.

"It's okay," he said softly, though his voice carried like a bell in the chamber. "It's time to unburden yourself. Speak your truth, Snow."

The words fell over her like balm and fire, gentle yet undeniable.

Snow's breath quivered as she clung to Doc's hands. For a moment she let herself draw strength from his calm, his unwavering steadiness anchoring her against the storm of voices. Slowly, she nodded, wiping the last of her tears with the back of her wrist.

Her eyes rose, heavy and uncertain, to the towering form of Anubis. The golden jackal's face remained fixed, unreadable, eternal. His silence pressed against her like a weight she could not escape.

Snow drew in a sharp breath, her voice trembling as she forced the words free.

"I am afraid," she whispered. "Afraid that I am not worthy. Afraid that I am not deserving of redemption."

Her voice cracked, but she went on.

"I have failed… in my faith, in my love, in blaming and hating God. I shattered everything that should have been sacred. And now—" her lips trembled, her hands tightening around Doc's, "—now I do not know if I can be saved at all. If I am worthy of it. If I will ever be."

The sacred chamber held her words, vibrating with their truth. Her confession spread like a tremor through the silence, echoing into every shadow, into every waiting flame.

The chamber held her words in stillness. The torches hissed. The Raven tilted its head, feathers rustling faintly.

Then Anubis moved. The golden jackal's head lowered, his gaze fixed wholly upon her. His voice, when it came, was deep and resonant, like stone grinding against eternity.

"Well done, Snow White."

The words rang through the chamber, final and absolute. And with them, the air shifted. In a single breath, Anubis and the Gatekeepers dissolved, their towering forms breaking like smoke into nothingness. The circle was gone. The chamber was still.

Snow staggered, her chest rising and falling in shuddered breaths. She looked down—

And saw Doc.

He stood before her, small hands lifted, and in them he cradled a glowing, pulsing shape. Her heart.

Snow's breath caught, her lips parting in awe and dread. But Doc only smiled, warmth in his eyes, his voice soft and sure.

"Your heart is ready to be weighed."

Her trembling fingers reached out. She took the heart into her own hands, feeling its weight, its warmth, its impossible reality.

Step by step, she walked toward the towering Scales. The Raven watched, head cocked, unblinking.

Snow lifted her heart, her hands shaking, and set it gently upon one of the golden pans.

The Scales groaned under the weight, the sound echoing like thunder in the vast chamber.

And then all was still.

Trial 6: Final Balance

"You do not stay angry forever but delight to show mercy. You will again have compassion on us; you will tread our sins underfoot and hurl all our iniquities into the depths of the sea."

Micah 7:18–19

The scales accepted her offering.

Her heart, still warm and glistening, rested upon the burnished beam. On the opposite side, a single ostrich feather gleamed—a shard of heaven's order, radiant and impossibly still.

The chamber hushed. Not a breath of torchlight flickered, not a whisper of stone groaned. Silence fell with such weight that Snow White could hear the rhythm of her own pulse echoing inside the void.

Then came the shift.

It was not movement of floor or wall but something deeper—like reality itself sliding sideways. The golden chamber blurred, rippling like water across glass. The scales before her shimmered, fractured, and then solidified again—yet the air tasted different, sharp, metallic.

Snow lifted her gaze.

What had once been the chamber now stood as its mirror—every pillar, every torch, every shadow inverted, as though she had stepped inside the reflection of her own judgment. Behind the scales, darkness stirred. Not emptiness, not void—*shadows*. They moved like things alive, writhing, restless, waiting.

Snow drew breath, steadying herself. For a moment, the chamber was utterly still… until the shadows began to lean forward, pressing against the veil of the mirror-world, testing its seams.

And then—silence again.

She knew the trial had begun.

From the stirring shadows, a shape emerged—heavy, primal, stitched together from the worst of all beasts. A crocodile's jaws glistened with saliva, lion's mane bristling with coarse hair, hippopotamus shoulders rippling with grotesque power. Her eyes burned like coals, unblinking, fixed on the trembling scales.

Ammit.

Snow's breath caught as the Devourer began her slow orbit. The scrape of claw against stone echoed, deliberate, dragging out the silence with each measured step. She circled once. Twice. A third time. Close enough that Snow could feel the heat of her breath brush her cheek, smell the fetid hunger rising from her throat.

The growl came first—low, deep, rattling in the chest like distant thunder. Then words seeped into the air, jagged and cruel, carried on that guttural vibration:

"You doubt your worthiness to be saved, little queen…"

Her monstrous jaw twisted in something like a smile, though the rows of teeth gleamed too wet, too sharp.

"You always hated what was weak… what was fragile. You spat at it. Feared it. Buried it."

Another circle. Claws scraped stone, slower now, savoring the moment.

"But tell me, Snow White… the one you hated most… was she not closer than you wished to admit?"

Ammit's words hung there, heavy as chains.

Snow's throat tightened, though no reply yet formed. She only felt the weight of the scales, the shadows pressing closer, and the Devourer's eyes gleaming with truth she did not want to face.

Ammit's growl deepened, echoing through the mirrored chamber. Her massive form drew nearer with every step, until her jaws hovered just above Snow's shoulder, teeth glistening.

"Would you like a chance," she hissed, voice rasping with hunger, "to face the evil you spent so long hiding from?"

Snow clenched her hands, her chest tight.

The Devourer prowled past her, tail dragging, claws striking sparks against the stone.

"You dreamed of it, did you not? To stand against her. To meet her gaze without crown or court to shield her. To make her bleed as she made you bleed."

Snow's eyes burned, though no tears fell. She swallowed hard, fighting the rising knot of old fury.

"Yes," she whispered at last. "Once, I wished for that chance. To face her. To destroy her with my own hands if I could."

Ammit stopped, head tilting, eyes gleaming red in the shadows.

Snow raised her chin, steady now. "But that time has passed. I no longer hold resentment for her. She no longer has power over me."

A rumble rolled from deep in Ammit's chest, neither laugh nor growl, but something in between. Slowly, her lips peeled back, revealing all her teeth.

"Is that so…?"

The shadows thickened. They bent and swayed as though something unseen pressed through their veil.

Snow's breath caught as the shape resolved—slender at first, then regal, draped in flowing velvet and steel. From the darkness emerged a woman, each step measured, deliberate, echoing against the mirrored chamber floor.

Snow's eyes widened. She knew that face. She had dreamed it in terror, woken gasping, her sheets soaked with sweat. It was the only earthly thing she had ever truly feared.

The Queen.

But not the haggard crone who had poisoned her. Not the twisted witch from whispered tales. No—this was her at her peak. In the full cruel bloom of her beauty, flawless and terrible. Skin like ivory, lips blood-red, eyes glittering like frozen emeralds that could cut through steel. Her crown gleamed with cruel perfection, every jewel casting shards of cold light into the chamber.

Snow saw the shift with her own eyes, the way the shadows had bent and folded to form her. *Hautwechsler,* she thought—one of the shapeshifters from the German tales whispered at firesides. A changeling of skin and soul.

The Queen's gaze met hers, and Snow felt her heart falter. Fierce. Beautiful. Cruel.

Her nightmares had walked into the chamber.

The Queen's heels clicked against the mirrored stone, each step echoing like the toll of a bell. She did not rush—no, she savored the long walk, letting her presence fill every shadow. At last she stopped before the scales, her cruel beauty haloed by the swirling dark.

Her lips curved, though it was no smile—more a baring of teeth beneath painted red.

"Well, well… the little lamb has wandered far."

Her voice poured like velvet over glass, sweet and sharp in the same breath.

"Far enough, it seems, to forget the blade behind the mirror."

She tilted her head, eyes narrowing as though peering straight into Snow's chest.

"Tell me—can you feel it still? The hatred? The blame you once laid at my feet?"

Snow flinched, but the Queen pressed closer, her words a dagger twisting.

"Poor little princess. Too afraid to face her demons alone. Too fragile to bear the weight of her own shadows. So she fashioned me into her monster—her nightmare to curse, to loathe, to whisper about in the dark."

The Queen's voice dropped low, venomous, each syllable coiled in cruelty.

"But here we are. At the end. And fate has been merciful after all… granting you your unspoken wish."

Her eyes blazed with cold fire as she leaned nearer.

"To stand against the one who ripped away your family. Who made you fear every shadow, every monster in the dark. At last, the lamb will meet her wolf."

Snow straightened, the echo of the Queen's venom still reverberating through the chamber. Her voice trembled at first, but her words rang true.

"I never hated you," she said, lifting her chin. "I pitied you. Time and time again you tried to kill me—your own niece—and yet you failed. Still, I forgave you. Again and again, I forgave."

For a heartbeat, silence.

Then the Queen laughed.

It was not the brittle laugh of a courtier, nor the hollow cackle of a hag, but something far deeper—rich, guttural, and merciless. It sank into the bones, cold and suffocating, the kind of sound that made the soul recoil.

"You think that is why you hated me?" she purred, eyes gleaming like poisoned emeralds. "No, little lamb. That was never the reason."

She stepped closer, her presence towering, shadows curling tighter around her form.

"Think back. Open your mind. Recall the night you smothered beneath silence, the memory you chained away. The night you truly wished for my death."

Snow's breath quickened, her heart hammering.

The Queen's voice dropped to a hiss, every syllable sharp as glass.

"The night you saw me slip poison into your mother's cup."

The chamber seemed to constrict, shadows closing in.

"Yes… feel it. That venom that once seared your veins in Apophis' lair? That was not his alone. That was yours—the fire of your hatred, the moment you longed to end me with your own hands."

The Queen's words wrapped around her like a noose, dragging Snow toward a truth she had never dared to face.

And then—silence again.

The Queen's words pried at Snow's mind, and the chamber spun. Darkness swallowed her, pulling her down into a memory she had buried so deep she once believed it a nightmare.

She was small again. A child. Bare feet padding against cold stone.

She pressed herself into a secret hole in the castle walls, hidden behind a heavy tapestry. From there, she peered through a narrow slit into her mother's chamber.

Her mother sat in quiet grace, scripture open upon her lap, lips moving in soft prayer. The glow of candlelight danced on her face, serene, untouched by suspicion.

And then—her aunt.

Tall, resplendent, a silhouette framed by shadow. Snow saw her hand, steady and deliberate, slip the vial's contents into the chalice. At that exact moment, a lightning bolt split the sky. For the briefest instant, the chamber flared white, and her aunt's cruel smile burned itself into Snow's vision like a brand.

Snow's little hands clutched at the stone, trembling. Her heart thundered in her ears. She wanted to scream, to burst from her hiding place—but fear strangled her. Her throat closed, no sound could escape.

She turned and fled, darting deeper into the hollow veins of the castle walls. The stone swallowed her sobs as she ran, praying the image would vanish, that it had not been real. But it clung to her, etched in fire and shadow.

Her mother never looked up. She never saw. She only kept reading scripture, her voice steady, holy words echoing against the storm outside.

And then—

The memory shattered.

Snow gasped, yanked back into the mirror-chamber of the scales, the Queen's eyes gleaming down at her with merciless satisfaction.

Snow staggered back, her breath ragged, the chamber spinning around her.

"No…" she whispered. "It was only a nightmare. A child's nightmare."

Her hands shook as the truth settled, heavy as iron. She had buried it, dismissed it, sealed it away as fantasy. Never once had she dared call it what it truly was. Not dream. Not vision.

Testimony.

Her chest tightened, horror choking her. *How had she allowed her mind to do it?* How had she silenced herself, convinced herself it was only shadow and storm?

The Queen—her aunt—had poisoned her own sister. Slain Snow's mother as scripture rang through the room, holy words still warm on her lips. The serpent had struck even as the prayer rose.

Snow's knees weakened. Her stomach lurched. And then—

The fire came.

Hatred surged through her veins, hotter than any flame, blacker than any storm. Fury rose like a tide, choking, burning. She hated her aunt with a venom so sharp it carved itself into her very bones.

But beneath it, another hatred seethed—turned inward. She loathed herself for the silence, for the years of blindness, for hiding behind stone while her mother died.

Her nails dug into her palms until blood welled. Her heart thundered.

Snow was furious. At her aunt. At herself. At the world that had allowed it to be.

A rumble shook the mirrored chamber as Ammit's voice cut through the storm of Snow's fury. She had drawn closer again, massive form prowling around her like a vulture circling a dying prey.

"Yes…" Ammit hissed, jaws dripping, eyes ablaze. "There it is. The venom. The hatred that has always slept beneath your skin. You feed me well, little queen. You always have."

Her laugh was a guttural roar, claws scraping stone as she prowled faster, hungrier.

"You wished her death that night. You wished to strike her down. You tasted vengeance, and you would have swallowed it whole, if only your hands had been stronger."

The words pressed in on Snow, heavy, choking—yet something within her shifted.

Her breath slowed. Her eyes lifted. And she saw.

This rage, this venom, this story of hate and hunger—it was not hers anymore. It belonged to another girl, a broken child hiding in stone walls. It belonged to the shadows, to the Devourer, to the mirror-world that sought to chain her soul.

But not to her. Not now. Not here.

Ammit's jaws snapped inches from her face, her roar rolling through the chamber.

"You are mine, little lamb!"

Snow's gaze did not falter. For the first time, she looked straight through the beast.

This was no longer her story.

No longer her wounds.

No longer her rage.

And in that truth, the chamber quaked.

Snow drew a long breath, the fire of rage still burning in her chest—but she did not let it consume her. She steadied her trembling hands and lifted her gaze to the Queen.

"I forgive you."

Her voice was not weak. It was not broken. It was steady—iron wrapped in velvet.

"Despite the evil you wrought. Despite the lives you stole. I forgive you. Not for your sake... but for mine."

The Queen froze. Her cruel smile faltered, her perfect face held motionless as though struck by something beyond her reckoning.

Ammit stopped mid-circle, claws locked against the stone, eyes narrowing. For the first time, the scales themselves shuddered. A low tremor rippled through the chamber, the golden beam rattling beneath the weight of heart and feather.

Silence stretched—tense, thick, unbroken.

Then Ammit's jaw split open, and she released a ravenous laugh. It rolled through the mirror-walls like thunder in a tomb, a sound so full of hunger it seemed to gnaw at the very air.

The chamber shook again. The shadows writhed, drawn by her delight.

The Queen's emerald eyes flickered as the scales rattled, as though something ancient had awakened at Snow's words. Slowly, her lips curled back into a smile—sharp, triumphant, edged with madness.

"Ahhh…" she breathed, spreading her hands as though to welcome an unseen audience. "They stir."

The shadows writhed higher, pressing against the mirrored walls, whispering with a thousand hidden tongues.

"Let them show it," the Queen crooned. "Let them bare the truth of your heart." Her voice rose in a fevered hymn, half-taunt, half-revelation. "The chamber itself shakes at your defiance. The lamb dares forgive the wolf."

Her gaze sharpened, snapping back to Snow with a cruel twist of her smile.

"But it seems…" she purred, tilting her head, "there is something missing."

She stepped closer, her beauty crueler than a blade, her shadow falling across Snow.

"One more deed… for the little lamb to do."

The words hung in the chamber, thick as blood, trembling with promise.

Snow's body stiffened, her shoulders locking as the Queen's words echoed.

"One more deed?" she whispered, dread thickening in her throat.

The Queen's smile widened, terrible in its beauty. Her voice dropped to a silken hiss, every word soaked in venom and promise.

"Do you long for peace, little lamb?" she purred. "Do you truly wish to balance the scales?"

The chamber groaned, the shadows pressing closer, as though they too leaned in to hear the verdict.

"There is only one way…" the Queen whispered, stepping nearer, her presence smothering. "You must kill the one who shattered it all. The one who stood silent in the dark. The one who did nothing."

Her eyes glowed, cruel and triumphant, as her words sank like daggers.

"The one who watched… and never spoke a word."

The scales rattled violently. The chamber quaked.

Snow's breath caught in her chest, the weight of the truth pressing down, threatening to crush her.

Snow's breath hitched, her heart hammering in her ears.

"The one… who did nothing?" she whispered, trembling.

The Queen's smile sharpened into a perfect blade. Her voice cut like silk drawn across a throat.

"Yes, little lamb." She leaned close, emerald eyes blazing. "The one who hid in the walls while her mother drank poison. The one who silenced her own tongue. The one whose fear left the door open for death to creep in. The one you hate most…"

Her words lingered, each syllable tightening around Snow's chest.

"…is you."

The chamber reeled. Snow staggered, the air itself pressing against her.

The Queen reached out with long, alabaster fingers, her nails gleaming like obsidian talons. Slowly, deliberately, she caressed Snow's cheek.

And then—she tore.

With a sickening sound, the Queen's flawless skin split and peeled, curling back like parchment under flame. She shed herself as a serpent sloughs its old husk. Strips of pale flesh unfurled, cracking, flaking, revealing what lay beneath.

Beneath the ruin, the face that emerged was no longer the Queen's. It was Snow's own. Perfect in form, radiant in cruelty, every feature sharpened into a merciless reflection.

She stood before her double—her mirror self, terrible and beautiful, every inch her equal.

Snow stared into her own eyes, and for the first time, it was not her nightmares she faced—

It was herself.

Ammit roared, the sound shaking the mirrored chamber like thunder beneath the earth. Her laughter rolled into ravenous snarls, eyes wide with fevered hunger. She reared back on her massive haunches, jaws gaping, saliva spilling in thick ropes as she slammed her claws against the stone.

"Yes!" she howled, her voice trembling with glee. "Yes! The truth—at last! The lamb is her own wolf! Her own executioner! Feed me, little queen! Feed me what is mine!"

The scales rattled violently, tilting under the weight of heart and feather as though the chamber itself might splinter. Shadows clawed at the walls, shrieking in tongues long dead.

From across the trembling chamber, Umbra-Snow reached to her side. With elegant precision, she drew forth a weapon that shimmered in the dark like a shard of steel moonlight.

A Katzbalger.

Its blade was broad and short, built not for elegance but for brutal efficiency. The guard curled into a protective figure-eight, forged in thick iron that gleamed with cruel promise. This was a sword meant for close combat, for flesh and bone, for survival in the press of bodies where

grace gave way to violence. The grip was leather-wrapped, worn smooth, yet steady—solid enough to never slip in blood.

The umbra smirked, holding the weapon out with a predator's grace. Then, with a flick of her wrist, she hurled it at Snow's feet. The clang of steel rang through the chamber like a death knell.

"Pick it up," she commanded, her voice Snow's own, yet colder, sharper, crueler.

Snow's double walked closer until she stood before her, the katzbalger gleaming at her feet like an executioner's gift. Her reflection tilted her head, eyes burning with mockery.

"Don't you want to know," she whispered, voice a venomous echo, "why the scales will not balance?"

Snow froze, breath shallow.

"They are waiting," The umbra purred, circling her like a predator, "for you to finish what must be done. Finish what you yourself confessed."

She leaned close, words a dagger in Snow's ear.

"You said it, didn't you? That you are not worthy. That you do not deserve redemption. So kill her—the part of yourself that you blame for every fracture, every shadow, every silence."

The chamber shook with her cruelty, shadows writhing, Ammit's growl thrumming beneath it all.

Umbra-Snow straightened, her smile sharp as broken glass.

"Naïve little lamb. They almost carved obedience into your tombstone. And yet you thought kindness would save you?"

Her laugh was low, guttural, Snow's own voice twisted into a cruel hymn.

"You still fancy yourself the fairest of them all?"

She stepped closer, her eyes aflame with accusation.

"You cannot wash your hands of blood with silence. You cannot speak pretty words into the void and hope they will blot out your guilt. You cannot profess forgiveness like a prayer and expect your scales to sway in mercy."

Her hand hovered above the blade, not touching, but commanding.

"The truth will not bow to your pity, little lamb. It demands sacrifice."

The katzbalger gleamed, waiting.

The umbra's smile curved wider, a serpent savoring the strike.

"You paraded your innocence like a crown," she cackled. "Flaunted your face and called it virtue. You let the dwarfs adore you because it was easier than facing a world that did not care who you were—only that you were beautiful."

She circled tighter, each word a lash.

"You wore beauty like a shield. But underneath it? Nothing. No spine. No flame. Just a coffin… waiting for a prince to kiss it."

She laughed then, sharp and guttural, a sound dripping with both amusement and disgust. The shadows quivered at the sound, Ammit's growl harmonizing in delight.

"And oh, that coffin," Mirror-Snow crooned, her voice rising in cruel song. "That glass prison. You laid there perfectly still, pretending you were dead. They wept for you. They worshipped you. And you didn't speak. You didn't scream. Because it was easier to be a story… than to be alive."

Her eyes blazed as she leaned forward, words striking like knives.

"Do you even know how long you were in there? How long they watched you—silent, frozen, preserved? You became a relic. A relic they could dress and adore and project their fairy tale onto."

The chamber pulsed with her laughter, shadows rippling like water disturbed.

The umbra's voice softened, venom dripping from each word.

"And worst of all…" she whispered, leaning close, emerald eyes alight with triumph, "…you liked it."

The words struck like a lash.

Snow's stomach churned, fury and fear colliding in her chest. This reflection—this cruel, perfect double—was everything she feared might live within herself. She loathed it, despised it, but the disgust twisted into something hotter, sharper. Rage.

At their feet, the katzbalger pulsed in the shadows, its steel glimmering as though it burned with unseen fire.

The umbra tilted her head, lips curling into a cruel smile.

"Be honest," she taunted, her voice Snow's own, twisted to mockery. "You don't want peace. You want vengeance. You want to destroy the part of you that was weak enough to lie in that coffin and call it salvation."

The chamber shuddered, the scales trembling, Ammit's growl rumbling like thunder.

And then—something within Snow lit. A spark deep and fierce, born of fury and shame, born of the fire she had tried for so long to bury.

She bent down. Her fingers wrapped around the hilt.

The sword's weight surged into her arm, heavy, unnatural. It was not like holding a weapon—it was like grasping a version of herself, a part of her soul she had locked away, chained in silence and fear.

Snow lifted the blade. Its steel gleamed, hungry.

Mirror-Snow's lips curved into a satisfied smile.

"There she is."

Ammit's monstrous maw split into a grin, jagged teeth flashing in ravenous delight. Her eyes gleamed red as she drank in the sight—the lamb finally lifting the blade against herself.

Snow lunged.

The katzbalger sang as it cut through the air, meeting its twin with a scream of steel. Mirror-Snow caught the strike, her own blade locked against Snow's, sparks leaping into the shadows.

The chamber erupted into violence.

It was no graceful duel of courtiers—no, this was survival's dance. Brutal, sharp, merciless. Two masters locked in combat, each knowing the other's every instinct, every feint, every weakness.

Steel rang. Blades crashed against the mirrored floor, glancing past throats, grazing flesh. Close calls left skin torn, blood dripping down pale wrists. Blunt strikes rattled bone, cruel blows left bruises blooming.

Every strike was mirrored, every step answered. It was like fighting one's own heartbeat, one's own breath, one's own shadow made flesh.

The chamber echoed with the clang of iron, the snarl of breath, the hiss of sweat and blood.

And still, neither gave ground.

Their blades locked, grinding against each other with a shriek of iron. Umbra-Snow leaned in, lips curling into a sneer as their faces hovered inches apart.

"You didn't scream when your mother fell," she spat. "Didn't move when the Queen whispered murder through the kingdom's halls. You watched—oh yes, you watched. A little girl... and you curtsied."

Snow roared and shoved her back, steel clashing in a storm of sparks. They circled, each strike answered with another, boots sliding across the mirrored floor. Blades hissed, slammed, tore chunks from the air itself.

Again the words came, cruel and cutting, sharper than the sword in her hand.

"You used your beauty like bait. You wanted to be admired... not known."

Snow's fury burned in her veins, but her reflection matched her pace, her rhythm, her rage.

Then came the strike.

The umbra pivoted with cruel precision, the katzbalger flashing like lightning. Snow gasped as steel carved into her arm, slicing through flesh. Blood spilled hot and bright, spattering across the mirrored stone.

The sting seared, but worse still was the smirk on her double's face.

Snow staggered back, clutching her bleeding arm, but her reflection gave her no quarter. Mirror-Snow advanced with relentless fury, blades sparking as she forced Snow onto her heels.

"You call yourself a survivor," she hissed, each word punctuated by a vicious strike. Their swords screamed together, the clash echoing like thunder.

"But what did you really survive?" A blow drove Snow sideways, steel biting dangerously close.

"The poison?" Another strike, cruel and fast, cutting sparks from the floor.

"The Queen?" A shove, the mirrored blade forcing Snow's guard down.

The umbra's eyes blazed with triumph as she pressed closer, her words more jagged than her steel.

"Or was it the shame? The shame of letting them all die for you?"

The words slammed into Snow harder than the blade itself. Blood dripped onto the mirrored stone, each drop ringing louder than steel.

Snow raised her blade, fury trembling in her wounded arm, ready to counterstrike—

And then the chamber fractured.

A scream tore from her throat as the mirrored floor rippled, and from the shadows came a shape. The first dwarf stumbled forward, his body bent and broken, limbs twisted grotesquely to match his name. His mouth hung open in a silent moan, eyes bulging, veins blackened as though poisoned by years of deformity.

"Sleepy…" Snow gasped, but the name curdled on her tongue.

He faded—only for another form to lurch into view. Bashful, his skin peeled raw and flayed, as though shame itself had stripped him bare. His face hid behind bloody fingers, and yet his sobs filled the chamber like a dirge.

"No—no!" Snow cried, stumbling back, her sword slipping in her grasp.

Another flicker. Another horror. Doc, ribs cracked open like the pages of a grotesque book, his heart missing, hollowed out. His mouth still moved, lips whispering wisdom with no breath behind them.

Snow screamed, clutching her ears, the chamber spinning.

Grumpy's silhouette appeared next, teeth shattered, lips torn in a permanent snarl, his body hunched as though beaten by centuries of anger. He lurched toward her, the sound of his growl guttural, inhuman.

"Stop! Please—stop!" Snow shrieked, breath tearing out of her lungs.

One by one, they appeared, mutilated reflections of love turned nightmare—each dwarf a corpse of their own name, each apparition dripping blood onto the mirrored floor, pooling around her feet.

Snow fell to her knees, the images strobing in and out of existence, her cries echoing in time with their fading groans.

And still, the illusions came.

Sneezy—his face bloated, nose shredded raw, throat torn open from coughing fits that had split him inside out. Mucus and blood dripped from him in sickening strings, every breath a death rattle.

Behind him came Dopey, his head twisted grotesquely on his shoulders, tongue lolling, eyes glassy and vacant. His limbs spasmed in jerks, like a puppet cut from its strings, drooling incoherence as he collapsed at her feet.

Snow gagged, bile rising in her throat.

Then came the seventh.

At first she prayed it wasn't him. That the shadows would swallow this last horror before she saw. But the shape stepped forward, and her heart shattered.

Happy.

But he was no longer joyful, no longer light. His face was split in a rictus grin, the flesh of his cheeks torn wide and stitched back grotesquely, a parody of laughter carved into skin. His eyes bulged with terror behind the mockery of a smile, tears of blood streaking down his face. His chest was ripped open, ribs broken back, as if someone had clawed his heart from within— yet his mouth kept grinning, stretching wider, wider, until it nearly split him in two.

Snow's scream broke into a sob as Happy staggered closer, dripping entrails and sorrow, the cruelest corpse of them all.

The chamber quaked with their grotesque parade, the air choking with the stench of rot and iron.

Snow's scream shattered into rage. She surged to her feet, the katzbalger flashing. With a fierce lunge she drove the blade low, steel biting deep into her reflection's calf. Blood sprayed across the mirrored floor, black-red against the glow of the scales.

Umbra-Snow staggered but laughed through clenched teeth, eyes gleaming with malice.

"There it is! The savior's truth!" she jeered. "You were supposed to be their light—and you let them rot in the ruins of a broken kingdom!"

Their blades clashed again, sparks raining like fire. They shoved, kicked, slashed—flesh torn, steel grinding, blood dripping with every breath.

Snow roared and swung hard, slamming the blunt end of her sword across her double's face. The crack resounded through the chamber, and blood streaked down Mirror-Snow's cheek.

Still, she only grinned wider. Her laugh was jagged, hungry, echoing in time with the scales' trembling.

"There she is. The real Snow White. Not the savior. Not a queen. Just a little girl who froze... and let the world fall apart."

The words hung heavier than the blood dripping to the floor.

Steel screamed. Shadows writhed. Then with a vicious strike, the umbra knocked the blade from her hand and drove her backward. Snow crashed hard against the mirrored floor, breath ripped from her lungs.

The chamber rang with laughter.

The umbra circled her fallen form, each step deliberate, her voice cutting through the silence like a lash.

"Of course you are on the ground. Weak."

Snow pushed to rise, but Ammit lunged. A clawed slash ripped across her leg, tearing flesh. She cried out, stumbling, blood trailing down her calf.

Umbra-Snow's voice rose, fierce and merciless, yelling over her gasps.

"You survived the apple."

Snow's hand shook against the stone.

"You survived the Queen."

The chamber tilted, shadows pressing closer.

"You survived the silence of the grave."

Snow gasped, dragging herself upward, her body trembling.

"But you never survived yourself."

Her reflection leaned down, emerald eyes blazing. "Tell me, Snow—what did your survival cost you? You lived. But others bled. Others burned. Others were buried."

Snow's vision blurred with pain and blood, the words cutting deeper than any wound.

The umbra's smile curved cruel as she shouted her final blow:

"But you—" she sneered, pointing at her trembling form, "you were kissed. You were worshipped. You were carried out in glass like a saint!"

The words reverberated in the chamber, louder than her scream.

The umbra crouched low, her face inches from Snow's, her bloodied smile stretching too wide. The blade in her hand gleamed as she pressed her words sharper than steel.

"You are to blame for her death."

Snow flinched, her body trembling, but the reflection's voice only grew stronger, echoing in the chamber.

"You watched. You saw the poison slip into her cup. And you said nothing."

The words pierced deeper than any wound. Snow gasped, the memory flashing again before her eyes—her mother's lips moving in prayer, the thunderbolt flashing, her aunt's shadowed smile.

"You let her die!" Umbra-Snow snarled, her voice breaking into a scream. "You let her murderer take the throne!"

Snow pressed her hands over her ears, shaking her head, but the words seeped through, venomous and unstoppable.

"You buried the truth in silence. You let her voice vanish beneath scripture. You let her crown fall into the hands of a serpent."

Snow's chest heaved, her throat closing around a sob.

"It is your fault!" The umbra roared, rising above her, arms spread wide as if delivering judgment. "You killed her as surely as if you poured the poison yourself!"

Snow's hands fell from her ears. Her eyes filled with tears, her body shaking as the weight of it crushed her.

"No…" she whispered, her voice breaking. "No… I… I am to blame. I am unworthy."

Her sword slipped in her trembling hand.

The scales above rattled violently, as if trembling in agreement.

The umbra moved slowly, almost tenderly, though cruelty dripped from every motion. She crouched beside Snow's trembling form, the mirrored floor slick with her blood.

Her hand shot out, fingers like iron, fisting in Snow's dark hair. She yanked her head back, hard enough that pain lanced down Snow's spine, her scalp screaming.

"Look at me," the reflection hissed.

Snow's eyes squeezed shut, tears streaming down her cheeks, breath ragged with grief. But the pull tightened, her neck straining until it burned, until she could not resist.

"Look," Umbra-Snow growled, forcing her face up toward the scales' shimmering light.

Through her tears, Snow saw herself—the twisted reflection, the face she both knew and loathed. Her double's lips curved in a cruel smile, eyes blazing with emerald fire.

Tears dripped hot and bitter down Snow's face, falling onto her bloodstained gown. She turned her head away with what little strength remained, but the fist in her hair jerked hard, wrenching her back.

"Look again!" The umbra barked, her voice rising into a scream. Her eyes locked onto Snow's like shackles snapping closed.

For a moment, time stilled. The chamber darkened, the scales rattled, shadows coiled like serpents. Only their two faces remained, reflections locked in merciless symmetry.

The double's smile sharpened, words curling in her throat like a blade poised to strike.

"I want you looking at me when I say this."

The umbra's grip on her hair tightened, forcing Snow's tear-streaked face higher as her voice dropped into a mocking hymn.

"Do you remember what they were?" she hissed. "Your father—mighty and brilliant—he tamed war with wit. He held a nation in the palm of his hand. Kings bowed to his counsel, armies bent to his will."

Her smirk widened, eyes burning like venomous jewels.

"And your mother… your mother was a queen of the people. Her crown was not gold but devotion. She gave her heart to them, every breath spent in sacrifice."

Snow sobbed, her chest heaving, but the words pressed on, relentless.

"And you?" Umbra-Snow spat. "You didn't even mourn her. You put her in the ground and let her murderer tuck you into bed. You are a mockery of your family name."

Her voice rose, cruel and thunderous, echoing against the mirrored walls.

"You think wearing your mother's crown makes you anything more than a shadow? That you could ever graze the edge of her strength? She ruled with grace while you cowered with a smile. She sacrificed while you survived. She isn't your legacy—you are her shame!"

The scales trembled, the chamber groaning as if recoiling from the words.

The umbra leaned in closer, her breath cold against Snow's ear, her voice dropping into a sickening, serpentine whisper.

"If only she could see you now—," she scoffed between each broken statement, "begging for meaning in a dead chamber of stone—," disdain in her laugh as she continued, "she would turn her back on you. Not because of what you lost…"

Her lips curled into a final, poisonous smile.

"...but because of what you never became."

Snow's voice cracked, raw with sobs.

"Please... stop..."

But her reflection's grip only tightened, jerking her head higher. The words struck sharper than steel.

"You are a burden, not a legacy. A silence, not a song. A child who let a kingdom rot because she could not bear to stand upright in her mother's shadow."

Snow whimpered, but the voice thundered on.

"And the truth—the cruel, final truth—" Umbra-Snow's emerald eyes burned with merciless triumph, "is that your mother would be ashamed of you. Ashamed of what became of her blessed child."

With that, her grip loosened. She released Snow's hair, and her head dropped forward, hanging low, shoulders trembling as tears streamed unchecked down her face.

But the words did not fade. They echoed, twisted, multiplied—rattling across the mirrored walls until they became a chorus of accusations. *Burden. Silence. Ashamed.*

Snow shook, broken beneath their weight.

Behind her, claws scraped stone. Ammit prowled closer, massive jaws parting, strands of saliva stretching between her fangs. Her nostrils flared, savoring the scent of weakness—the scent of her next victim, so close, so ready to be served.

Snow's chest heaved. She could hardly catch her breath. She was drowning again—defeated, weak, crushed under her reflection's merciless truth.

She pressed her trembling hands to the floor, desperate to steady herself, to hear something other than the endless echo of her own shame.

And then—soft, fragile, almost too faint to be real—

"...Snow..."

Her name. A quiet call, threading through the shadows like a whisper of light.

Snow's breath hitched. At first, she thought the call came from the chamber itself, some faint mercy carried on the air. But as she stilled, listening through the echoes of shame, she knew—

It wasn't outside her.

It was within.

The voice rose from the deepest place in her soul, a hidden well she had long forgotten. Fragile, but steady. Quiet, but unwavering. It carried no accusation, no cruelty—only her name, spoken with love.

"...Snow..."

And with it came warmth.

It spread through her chest, small at first, a flicker against the frost. Then it grew, like spring breaking through the grip of winter, thawing what had been frozen, softening what had been stone.

Snow closed her eyes. Tears still streaked her face, blood still marked her skin—but in the darkness behind her eyelids, the warmth pulsed brighter. Stronger. Calling her deeper.

The chamber fell away.

And she was ripped into memory.

***

The stone floor was gone.

The sword. The scales.

All vanished.

Snow was a child again. Five years old, small and brimming with questions, her legs dangling from the side of her mother's throne — the very seat the queen allowed her to climb into when the court had emptied and the day drew to a close.

Her mother sat beside her. Not armored. Not crowned. But radiant in quiet beauty. Her hair fell loose, her smile was soft, and the last gold of the setting sun streamed through the high glass windows, catching fire in her eyes.

She turned toward her daughter, as though she had been waiting here all this time.

"Do you know something, my little star?"

The child Snow shook her head.

The queen's hand lifted to her daughter's cheek, and her touch was warm.

"Before you were even born… I knew you."

Snow looked up at her, wide-eyed.

"I could feel you waiting," her mother whispered, her voice trembling not with sorrow but with awe. "Out there, beyond the veil of this world. My daughter. My miracle. I prayed for you — and I felt you pray back."

Her words fell like light across the chamber.

"And when you came to me, tiny and perfect, I knew why I had lived. You are the lifeline to my heartbeat, Snow. The rhythm of every breath I take. The melody in every song I've ever heard."

A shiver passed through Snow. She remembered this. The moment long forgotten but undeniably real.

"You are more than what this world will ever say about you," the queen said. "You are mine. And that is enough."

She leaned forward, resting her forehead to her daughter's, just as she had done when the storms howled outside and only a mother's nearness could calm them.

"And when I am gone," she said softly, "when the night grows long… remember this: You were never made to be perfect. You were made to rise."

Snow looked into her mother's eyes — and in them she saw not the image of a queen, but the truth of a mother.

And in that instant, she understood.

This was the moment.

This was the gift she had been carrying all along.

Not a sword.

Not a title.

 Not even a name.

But love.

Unshaken. Undeniable. Eternal.

***

When Snow's eyes opened, the chamber of the scales swam back into focus. The shadows still writhed, Ammit still circled, her reflection still loomed before her—but something had changed.

Her body screamed with pain. The slashes along her arm and leg burned, blood dripping steadily onto the mirrored floor. Every breath was ragged, every muscle trembled with exhaustion. She was cut, battered, bleeding—but no longer hollow.

Something within her had opened.

Her gaze fell to her hands—once small, once trembling. Now she saw not only her own bloodied fingers but the warmth of another's layered there, soft and steady. The child she had been, sitting beside her mother in prayer, waiting all these years to be remembered.

It struck her with sudden clarity: she owed that child more than vengeance. More than grief. She owed her the strength to rise.

Snow drew in a long, steadying breath.

She knew what she had to do.

She had to rise.

She had to face the thing she feared most.

She had to finish this.

Snow's breath came back in pieces—shallow at first, then steadier, as though her lungs had remembered something long forgotten. With trembling hands pressed to the mirrored floor, she began to push herself upward.

She rose as the queen she once was, crowned in a kingdom of frost and shadow.

She rose as the pilgrim who had walked the depths of the Duat, scarred but unbroken.

And she rose as the little girl who had waited in silence, patient and unseen, for this moment to shine through and be resurrected.

Her mirror self sneered, circling, the blade still dripping with blood.

"Well, well," she crooned, her voice sharp and mocking. "The little bird still has some fight in her. What will she say for herself now?"

Snow said nothing.

The reflection's laugh cracked through the chamber, venomous, hungry.

"Come on," she jeered, leaning in closer, taunting. "Beg. Proclaim. Defy. Show me what you are."

But Snow's silence was louder than words. One foot pressed beneath her, then the other, her body shuddering with pain but unwavering.

She was rising. Resolute. Quiet.

The chamber trembled with her ascent.

Umbra-Snow's smirk fractured into fury. Her emerald eyes blazed as she stepped closer, circling like a predator denied its kill.

"Speak!" she snarled, her voice echoing off the mirrored walls. "Defend yourself! Say *something!*"

Snow only straightened further, her body trembling but her gaze steady.

Her reflection leaned so close their noses nearly touched, her voice a hiss dripping with venom.

"Say it! Prove you are more than a coward's shadow!"

Snow's lips trembled. For a moment she looked as though she might break again—then the words rose from her chest, shaky but fierce, her voice cracking through the chamber- that little girl within choosing to rise one last time.

"While there is truth in all the venom you have spit…" she said, tears streaking her cheeks, "despite any wrongs I did… I was loved."

Her reflection faltered, eyes narrowing.

Snow pressed on, her breath quivering but her words sharpened by conviction.

"I was loved on purpose, and with purpose. I was loved before I was even in my mother's womb. I was made for her. I was made to be Snow White."

Her voice caught, choking on grief and defiance all at once. She closed her eyes, tears falling heavy, before her last words broke free like a cry torn from the soul:

"I was loved deeply. And anyone worthy of that kind of love… is worthy of redemption."

The chamber quaked, her words reverberating like a hymn against stone.

A sound filled the chamber. Not the grinding of metal, not the clatter of weight, but something higher, purer. The scales rang with music—soft, elegant, radiant. It was not sound. It was release.

The beam steadied. Heart and feather aligned. The scales balanced.

Then came the crack.

A sharp, distant sound vibrated through the mirrored walls as fissures splintered across the chamber's reflection. The illusion trembled, spiderweb lines spreading outward. Mirror-Snow's form shuddered, her cruel smile flickering before splitting away entirely.

In her place stood Ma'at.

At last, Snow saw her true form—majestic, serene, radiant with order. The goddess of truth and balance, unveiled at last. Ma'at met her gaze and inclined her head in a single, solemn nod. Approval. A judgment passed.

And then, as swiftly as a breath, Ma'at vanished. Ammit with her.

The chamber fell still. The shadows silenced. The air held its breath.

Snow stood alone before the scales—bloodied, aching, trembling.

Then she heard it.

Laughter.

Gentle, warm, familiar laughter that rippled through the silence like sunlight breaking a storm. She turned sharply, her heart racing, and there he was—standing just behind the scales.

Happy.

Hands folded across his round belly, cheeks full and ruddy, eyes sparkling like sunlit cider. His smile was the first true thing she had seen in what felt like a lifetime.

"Well," he chuckled, tilting his head, "you sure took your time."

A Walk With Happy

He stood there as if the nightmare had never happened.

The air still smelled of ash and blood. The walls pulsed with the heat of memory, the aftershocks of pain not yet finished echoing through the floor. But in that moment, the ruin receded—because he was there.

Happy. Whole. Undistorted. Himself.

Snow did not hesitate. She ran.

Her boots struck the obsidian floor, scattering the last of the horrors like smoke in sunlight. She crossed the space between them, nearly tripping over her own exhaustion, and threw herself into his arms.

He caught her without flinching.

He held her as if she were something precious and intact, as if she hadn't just clawed her way through madness—as if she hadn't just seen every person she loved torn apart.

She buried her face in the crook of his shoulder and inhaled. He still smelled like pinewood, warm stone, and a memory she couldn't quite catch—like the first time she saw morning after the forest stopped feeling safe.

He chuckled softly. There was something different in him now. Not broken—but burnished. The kind of joy that had walked through grief and stayed behind anyway, stubborn as sunrise. The kind of joy the world could never give—and so the world could never take away.

He pulled back slightly and looked at her with quiet wonder.

"Look at you," he said gently. "You've walked through fire. Spoke truths that scorched your tongue. You faced shadows with nothing but the light God placed in you before you were born. And still… your heart didn't break."

Snow tried to respond, but her throat closed around the words.

"I'm proud of you," he said. "Truly. We all are. But me?" He smiled, and it wasn't just joy—it was faith made flesh.

"I'm proud like someone who knows what it means to walk through the valley of the shadow of death and fear no evil. Because I see now—goodness and mercy have followed you, even when you couldn't feel them."

Her breath caught. His words wrapped around her like scripture written in stars.

He lifted her chin slightly, his thumb gentle under her jaw. "You've been pressed, but not crushed. Struck down, but not destroyed. That's not just strength, Snow... that's grace."

His words fell over her like the hush after thunder.

But still she shook. Her arms clung to him tighter, not from joy—but from the ache still caught in her chest.

They were gone now—the illusions—but their images clung to the back of her eyes like oil on water.

Grumpy's smile carved into a mask.

Doc's severed hands shaking on the altar.

Happy himself, hung by his own name.

She pulled back slightly. Her voice cracked. "I saw them die."

He didn't correct her. Didn't tell her it wasn't real.

He just nodded, slow and sad. "I know."

"They were... twisted. Torn apart. Turned into things they never were. And it felt like it would never end. Like it was truth."

He laid a hand over her heart. "That wasn't truth. That was torment."

His eyes held hers—and behind their warmth, something sharper gleamed. Righteous. Protective.

"That was the Accuser. The thief who comes to steal, kill, and destroy. He wanted to rob you of your memory. Turn your love into fear. Your loyalty into shame. He wanted to make you believe joy was a lie and grief was your only inheritance."

"It felt like it was," she whispered.

"Of course it did. The devil's always been good at counterfeits. That's why it hurt so much—because it almost looked like them. But what you saw wasn't your dwarfs. That was despair dressed in their skin."

Her lips trembled. "It felt eternal."

He leaned closer. His forehead touched hers.

"Evil always feels eternal when you're inside it. But it's not. It breaks. It has to. Because it was never meant to last."

"And what is?" she asked.

"Love," he said, without pause. "Joy. Faith. Hope. The things that don't make sense in hell—but still bloom there anyway. That's how you know they're real."

He exhaled slowly, voice quiet now, reverent. "What you saw was darkness trying to unmake you. And you stood up anyway. That's why I'm here."

He took a breath and looked around the blackened chamber, then back to her.
"But you're not done yet, little dove."

Her eyes narrowed. "There's more?"

He smiled again, but it didn't reach his eyes. Not this time. "There's truth, Snow. The kind you were never meant to carry alone. And it's time you see it—not through your pain, not through your fear... but through me."

He offered his hand. She hesitated, then slid her fingers into his. His grip was gentle—but it anchored her, as if he carried the calm of oceans beneath his skin.

The world around them rippled.

Light bloomed in the cracks of the obsidian, seeping through like veins in stained glass. The chamber softened, stretched, then split into something else entirely—not a place, but a remembrance.

The air turned pale. Cool. Fragrant like the incense of old temples.

The chamber was exactly as Snow remembered it in her nightmares—her mother's bed draped in velvet, the scent of rain drifting through the window shutters, and the scripture resting open on her lap as she whispered her evening prayers. Lightning shattered the night sky, and in its cold brilliance Snow saw again what she had been forced to bury: the silhouette of her aunt, dark and deliberate, pouring poison into the cup.

The vision held steady this time, no longer just a dream. Snow's throat tightened as she watched her younger self stumble back into the shadows, too frightened to speak, too small to stop it.

Her voice, older now, broke into the stillness. *"I ran. I saw her hand tip the poison, and I ran. I hid it away like a coward. And when the years passed, I convinced myself it had only been a dream. Better to believe a dream than the truth—that my silence killed her."*

She lowered her head, shame thick in her words. *"I never told a soul. I carried it like rot in my heart."*

But Happy, standing beside her, shook his head. For once his smile was not wide with cheer, but tempered and gentle, his eyes warm with something weightier than joy. He spoke softly, *"That is not why we are here, Snow. You've carried this shadow long enough. I've come to show you what came after."*

The air shifted, and the chamber began to tremble, the edges of the memory ready to fall away.

The memory shifted forward an hour into that storm-heavy night. The door opened, and Snow's father entered, his voice hushed, tender as he stepped toward the bed.

"My love, how went your prayers with your sister this eve?"

But no answer came. His brow furrowed. He drew nearer, watching for the gentle rise of her chest. None came. In a single, desperate motion he leapt across the chamber, falling to his knees at her side, pressing his ear close, searching with trembling fingers for her breath, her pulse. Silence.

A cry ripped from him, raw and kingly all at once: *"Guards! Physicians! Come at once!"*

The chamber flooded with life—guards pounding in, physicians hurrying to the bedside, courtiers and family rushing in behind, the queen's sister among them, cloaked in a mask of horror. And beside her, to Snow's astonishment, came Grumpy—his face pale, his eyes wide, as though the grief were his own to bare.

But the younger Snow, the child of this memory, was not there. She lay in her own bedchamber across the hall, tear-streaked and trembling. Servants hushed and rocked her, telling her it was only a dream. The king had commanded it so. She was not to see her mother's body cold upon the bed. He would bare that grief alone, mourning beside his wife through the night before her body was taken away.

And the older Snow—the one standing with Happy now—watched in stunned silence as both visions lived before her eyes: her father's despair, her aunt's false mourning, and Grumpy's presence beside them all.

Her breath faltered. *"Why was he there?"*

The memory stilled, waiting for Happy's answer.

Happy gave Snow only a quiet nod, his eyes telling her that her question must wait. The memory surged forward, the scene shifting into hours that passed like the sweep of a tide. The chamber was restless with movement—guards exchanging shifts at the doors, courtiers whispering behind sleeves, the royal family hushed in tense murmurs.

At last, the physician stepped forward, bowing his head low to the king. All sound in the chamber drained away, until only his voice remained.

"Your Majesty… it must have been from the injuries she sustained when the princess was born. Lingering, hidden all these years, until at last they claimed her life. There is no other explanation—for the Queen was in perfect health otherwise."

As he spoke, his eyes flickered—not to the king, but sideways, to the Queen's sister. The glance was fleeting but sharp, and Snow, watching, saw the truth in it: a pledge of loyalty, a promise of silence, a hope for reward.

The king, fighting to master his grief, looked downward, his shoulders trembling beneath the weight of a sorrow he dared not unleash before the court.

Snow's gaze was drawn across the chamber. There, apart from the others, stood Grumpy. His tears were real—cutting raw trails through the lines of his face—as he moved nearer the Queen's sister. His grief seemed unguarded, but there was something else.

A faint twitch of his nose. His breath hitched on the barest whiff.

Snow saw his eyes flicker sideways though his body remained rigid, feigning stillness. His gaze slid to the prayer table, to the Queen's cup left untouched by all but her hand. There— almost invisible, catching the faintest light of the torches—lay a powdered ring clinging to the rim.

Monkshood. Wolfsbane.

Snow's heart tightened. She knew what Grumpy knew: a tea cup settled with monkshood would send a woman to her grave before the poison had time to whisper its pain. Grumpy, with no word spoken, kept the secret in his eyes alone.

The king's voice, hollow and broken, cut through the murmurs.

"Leave us. All of you. Leave."

There was no argument in his tone, only command stripped bare of life. The court obeyed, shuffling reluctantly toward the door, the chamber emptying of physicians and courtiers, of family and guards. The latch shut behind them with a final echo.

Silence.

Then the storm broke loose within the king. His hand seized the nearest table, hurling it against the stone wall. Candlesticks and scripture scattered across the floor. Another vase shattered, splintering into shards that clattered like broken

prayers. His fury gave way to collapse, his knees striking the floor as his head lifted to the rafters.

A scream ripped from his chest, raw and primal, a sound of a man torn asunder, reverberating against the vaulted ceiling until his voice broke and left him trembling.

At last, he dragged himself to the bed. With shaking hands he drew back the covers and climbed beside her. He pressed his face into her hair, breathing in the last fading warmth of her scent, clinging to the familiar softness as if it might anchor her spirit to his own. His arms wrapped around her still body, desperate to keep her warm, to will her heart to beat again. And there, through the long night, he let his love hold the chamber. One final night. One final storm.

***

The vision shifted. The Queen's sister stormed down the corridor toward her chambers, a mask of dramatized grief painted across her features. She rushed past a shadow in the hallway—Grumpy—never even seeing him in her performance.

But as she swept by, his hand instinctively reached out, brushing the air as though to steady her. And in that instant, the faintest wisp touched his senses.

The same bitter trace. The same fatal perfume that had clung to the Queen's glass.

Monkshood.

It drifted from the folds of the sister's gown.

Grumpy froze, his breath caught, his body locked where he stood. His grief tangled with horror as the truth struck him silent.

The moment froze on Grumpy, standing stricken in the corridor, the poisonous scent curling off the Queen's sister. And then, as if pulled by the weight of memory, his mind carried him backward—years before, to a brighter time.

The royal gardens stretched wide beneath a gentler sun, the air sweet with blossoms and trimmed hedges. A girl of seven ran wild among the paths, skirts tangling around her ankles, her laughter ringing like bells. The younger sister—carefree, reckless, untouchable in her own belief.

Grumpy followed at a steady pace, his arms crossed, his gruff voice carrying a low chuckle. *"Foolish little thing… no fear in those bones of yours, eh?"*

She twirled, ignoring him, daring the world itself to bend to her will. For that day he was her companion, her guard, though he knew she would have called him her plaything if she could. And though he never said it aloud, she was his favorite among the royals. Always had been, since the moment she was born.

She had him wrapped around her finger. Every whim, every command, he yielded to with a grumble and a shake of the head.

Then his chuckle died. His eyes caught the patch ahead.

Monkshood.

The girl was running straight for it.

"Stop!" he barked, lunging forward. His arms caught her just before she stumbled into the violet stalks, and he swung her back gently but firmly.

She stared up at him, wide-eyed, breathless from the surprise. There was no fear in her gaze, only demand: she wanted to know what danger had dared come so close to her.

Grumpy knelt low, his face serious. His voice lowered into something weightier than usual, almost reverent.

"This, little one, this is monkshood. A flower as beautiful as it is deadly. To some, it can be medicine—used with care, in the right hands. But mishandled..." He plucked a withered leaf from the ground and crumbled it in his palm. *"...and it becomes poison. Wolfsbane. Strong enough to kill a man, or send a woman to her grave before she even feels it."*

Her eyes lingered on the blossom, a flicker of intrigue sparking in them even as her lips murmured thanks.

Grumpy frowned. Something in her curiosity chilled him, even then.

***

The storm-light flickered across Grumpy's face as he stood frozen in the corridor, the poisonous trace still heavy in his nose. His heart pounded. He could not let it go. He had to know.

He turned and bolted after her.

Her skirts swept around the corner ahead of him, her shadow darting into her chamber. Grumpy pushed forward, his steps echoing against the stone until at last he burst through the door. He slammed it shut behind him, chest heaving.

She stood before her mirror, hands pressed to her face in feigned despair. But when she caught sight of him in the reflection, the mask slid away. Her shoulders straightened, her hands fell, and her eyes turned to him—hard, glacial, merciless.

"What did you do?" Grumpy demanded, his voice cracking with disbelief. *"Tell me you didn't…"*

Her lips curved, not in grief but in cruel triumph.

"Do you remember," she said, her tone silken, *"the gardens? Do you remember who first taught me of monkshood? Who bent low and whispered of its beauty, its danger, its power? You told me, Grumpy. You."*

The words struck like a lash, and he staggered back, shaking his head.

"No… no, I never—"

"You did." Her voice cut sharper than the storm. *"And I listened. You think me a fool? I remember every word. It was you who directed my hand, whether you meant to or not."*

Her eyes narrowed, a venomous gleam flashing in them. *"Leave this place. I will grant you this mercy once—for old loyalty's sake. You are the only soul in this wretched court who will be spared my bite. Go. While you can."*

Grumpy's breath caught. His hands trembled at his sides, fury and heartbreak warring in silence. Then, with a strangled cry, he turned and fled.

Down corridors lit with torchlight, out the gates of the castle, into the darkened forest where the storm still wept. He ran until the stone gave way to earth, until the trees swallowed him whole. Magic lingered there, dancing upon every leaf, every drop of rain.

At last, he stumbled into the clearing, to the small wooden shed he had built as refuge. The very place Snow would one day know as part of the cottage.

The storm bent low over the forest as Grumpy stumbled into the shed. Rain drummed on the roof, and the little wooden walls seemed to groan beneath the weight of his grief.

He staggered to the shelves—those his friend had helped him build only last winter—and ripped them from the wall. Bottles shattered, tools clattered to the dirt floor. His voice rose in a ragged shout, breaking against the beams.

Blasphemies. Cries. Pleas to gods that would not answer.

And then, from the corner of the shed, a warmth stirred. Happy emerged, stepping quietly into the storm of grief. His eyes were not bright with mirth now, but soft, heavy with sorrow.

He reached out, and Grumpy fell into his arms. The dwarf's body shook as a howl tore from his chest—raw and unending. He wailed and wailed, clinging to Happy as though the world itself were crumbling beneath him.

Minutes passed before his voice broke enough for words.

"I told her," he gasped, his face buried against Happy's shoulder. *"The gardens… the monkshood… I told her everything. Fool that I am—I put the poison in her hand, and now… now she has murdered the Queen. I cannot go back. I can never go back!"*

His legs gave way, and he sank to the dirt floor. His fists beat against the earth, then opened, trembling, as though even his strength had abandoned him.

The shed was silent but for his sobs. Outside, the entire forest seemed to still, the leaves bowing low, the air turning cold—as though the trees themselves mourned with him. The breaking of his heart sent a chill through the roots of the world.

The vision of the shed dissolved into stillness. Happy stood beside Snow, his eyes resting on the memory of Grumpy as though seeing a brother long lost.

"Grumpy was no stranger to your family, Snow," Happy began softly. "He was not a bitter wanderer then, but a frequent presence in the castle, counted among the court. He was there the day your mother was born. And he was there again when your aunt first entered the world. From her very beginning, he gave her a devotion deeper than any vow."

Happy's voice lowered, almost reverent. "It was she who gave him the name you know him by. Grumpy. And once spoken, it clung to him more tightly than any before. That is how it is with us. Every hundred years or so, a new name is given. A word born from another's lips, a reflection of how they see us. And once it takes root… it becomes who we are for that century."

His eyes turned back to Snow, kind but weighted with sorrow. "Your aunt named him. And so—for a time—he was hers."

Happy's eyes lingered on the memory of his brother, his voice lowering into something gentler.

"After that night, Grumpy never returned to the castle. His heart was shattered, his faith in himself broken. But I could not let him vanish into the forest forever. I went to him, again and again, until at last he agreed to come with us. To join us in the mines. To bury his grief beneath stone and labor, where the world could not find him."

The memory shifted. Years passed in the space of a breath, and the shed once more stood before Snow's eyes. But now it was no longer the night of her mother's death. The storm had long since faded, replaced with the dim glow of lamplight from years later.

Snow recognized it immediately. The night she herself had come seeking refuge among the dwarfs.

Inside the shed, Grumpy stood with his back to the door, his voice low and sharp, speaking to Happy.

"We can't keep her here," he growled. *"If the Queen finds her, she'll slaughter us all. I won't carry that burden, Happy. I won't have her blood on my hands. Not again. Not hers, and not her mother's. Two generations of royals destroyed because of my folly—I'll not let it be me who curses the line a second time."*

His face twisted, torn between anger and despair, his fists clenching at his sides.

Snow's breath caught as she watched, hearing the bitterness she had once mistaken only for cruelty.

Grumpy's voice cracked through the shed like an axe striking stone.

"I won't have her blood on my hands, Happy! Not again. I won't carry it. Better she be gone from here than her death be counted against me. I cannot bear two generations lost!"

His words trembled between rage and despair, his face turned away, shadowed by the lamplight.

Happy stepped forward, his own tone quiet but unyielding. *"There is no other choice, brother. Cast her out now and she will not see another sunrise. The forest will claim her before dawn. You know this as well as I."*

Grumpy opened his mouth to protest, but his words were drowned by a sudden sound—sharp and unearthly.

A raven's caw split the air.

Both dwarfs stilled, their eyes lifting to the beam overhead where a black form sat in shadow, its feathers catching the lamplight in shades of midnight blue. The cry echoed with something deeper than birdcall, a note of omen, of fate.

Snow—watching the memory unfold—snapped her head to Happy. For there, perched upon his shoulder, sat the same raven. As though it had been with him all along. Its eyes gleamed, familiar and knowing, the very twin of the companion that had followed her through her Pilgrimage.

Her breath caught, and a spark of suspicion flickered in her gaze.

Happy turned to her then, his smile softened, his eyes steady with weight untold. "There was always more to Grumpy's story than bitterness, Snow. He was not what he seemed to you."

He held her eyes, the warmth in them deep as the roots of the world. *"Everything is connected."*

The words lingered, and before Snow could reply, the memory dissolved into brilliance.

She now stood before a great stone door, tall and arched, its surface carved with flowing patterns of stars and vines. The stone itself seemed to glow faintly, as though lit from within, warm and welcoming. Golden light traced the edges of the carvings, breathing life into them like veins of fire beneath the rock.

The air around her was still, hushed, yet not heavy—there was no dread here. Only calm, and the quiet anticipation of what lay beyond. The door did not threaten; it beckoned.

Happy stepped forward, the glow of the stone door painting his round face in soft gold. He turned to Snow, his eyes alight with warmth and pride.

"Snow," he said gently, "you have arrived at your final trial. You need only remember all that you have gained along your pilgrimage. Every step, every wound, every truth—it has brought you here."

He paused, then glanced to his shoulder, where the raven perched, its black feathers gleaming like polished obsidian. "What do you think? Is she ready?"

The raven gave a sudden flurry, wings ruffling in a delighted burst, feathers catching the golden light like sparks.

Happy's laughter rang out, bright and unburdened, the sound of sunlight breaking through storm clouds. With a twinkle in his eye, he lifted his hand and gestured toward the door.

The carvings seemed to breathe, light spilling gently from their etched lines, as though the door itself was alive and waiting for her touch.

Trial 7: Riddle to the Reeds

"You will seek me and find me, when you seek me with all your heart."

Jeremiah 29:13

Snow stood before the stone door, her heart still echoing with Happy's laughter and his gentle words. The raven ruffled its feathers in eager silence. For a long breath she lingered, hand trembling against the carved surface, before she pressed it open.

A hush fell.

The doorway revealed a stair that spiraled upward into shadow and light, each step wrought of stone so pale it gleamed like bone. It was no ordinary stair, but one alive with its own pulse—constellations shimmered faintly in its veins, as though she climbed not stone, but the very spine of the heavens. The higher she looked, the more the stair seemed to rise beyond measure, disappearing into veils of starlight.

Snow set her foot upon the first step.

The sound was swallowed whole, as though the Tower itself breathed her forward. Her ascent was slow, reverent. With each step, the weight of her pilgrimage pressed upon her shoulders, yet she felt lighter—as though sorrow and grief shed themselves behind her, rung by rung, like discarded cloaks. The air smelled faintly of parchment and incense, mingled with

a sweetness she could not name, and somewhere far above came the whisper of turning pages, like the wings of unseen angels.

The raven followed, a dark shadow circling upward around the stair's hollow heart. Once, its wing brushed a torch-bracket, and the flame flared into a star.

Snow's hand trailed the wall as she climbed, fingers brushing glyphs etched into the stone. They shifted beneath her touch—sigils of crowns, of swords, of scales, of hearts—all the trials she had endured flickering in and out of being as though the Tower itself remembered her journey. Higher and higher she went, until the stair ended at a great archway glowing with a light neither sun nor fire, but something purer.

Snow stepped through.

The chamber opened around her like the unfurling of a universe. Columns soared upward into darkness, dissolving into constellations that spun slow and patient in the vaulted heights. Between them, shelves upon shelves wound in endless spirals, each heavy with scrolls and tomes bound in every color of eternity. The very air hummed with breath and memory, a symphony of voices whispering as if all the world's stories spoke at once.

It was no mournful sound, but a hymn of triumph. Each whisper sang of a soul that had endured its own pilgrimage, had faced its final trial, and was written forever into this tower's keeping. Snow closed her eyes and felt it wash over her—the laughter of the redeemed, the sighs of the steadfast, the gentle weeping of those who had been found worthy. Euphoric bliss trembled in every note, each voice a champion crowned by the truth of their own heart.

Her gaze drifted higher. The shelves climbed past sight, and yet beyond them, further still, constellations gleamed, arranged not as random stars but as records of lives long extinguished, now set in the heavens like scripture. She realized with a sharp intake of breath— this tower held the records of every life since the first dawn, since creation itself.

The floor beneath her glowed faintly, etched in living starlight. As she walked forward, the constellations shifted, mirroring her own story: an apple bright as blood, her family's crest wrought of flame and silver, and finally, petals unfurling into the eternal geometry of the Flower of Life.

And at the chamber's heart stood the lectern.

Carved of obsidian veined in gold, it pulsed with a steady glow, as though it were alive. Upon it rested a scroll, blank as untouched snow, and beside it a quill of black feather tipped in molten light. Behind the lectern stood a figure robed in twilight—tall, ancient, with the head of an ibis and eyes like pools of endless ink.

Thoth, scribe of the cosmos.

To the right of the lectern, on a dais of red stone, crouched the Sphinx, vast and silent, her mane haloed by the glow of a ruby crystal the size of a man's chest. Atop the crystal perched the Raven, feathers glinting as if stitched from midnight fire. Its head tilted at Snow's approach, and she thought she saw in its dark eye the gleam of expectation.

The whispers stilled. The chamber breathed. All eyes, mortal and divine, were upon her.

The ibis-headed god stirred, feathers of inked shadow rippling about him as he stepped from behind the lectern. His staff rang softly against the starlit floor, a sound like quills scratching across endless parchment. When he spoke, his voice was not one voice but a thousand—layered whispers, chants, and songs, as though all the ages echoed through his throat.

"I am Thoth," he said, "scribe of the eternal. All that has been, all that shall be, passes through my hand. I weigh not the heart, nor judge the soul—for that belongs to others. My task is the record. The scroll. The remembrance."

He lifted the quill, holding it aloft as its tip flared like a falling star.

"Yet know this: not every life finds its way here. The shelves of this tower are vast, but not infinite. The stories inscribed are those sealed by truth, etched by faith. When a soul reaches the end of its pilgrimage, if it cannot face the truth of what it is, if it will not answer with the honesty of its heart, then no record can be written. Such a life is unpenned, and drifts into silence. Forgotten."

His gaze, dark and fathomless, fell upon Snow.

"You have endured trials of crown and serpent, of blood and scales, of shadow and mirror. You have been weighed and burned, broken and raised. But still your story lies unwritten. Only you may inscribe it. Only you may speak your truth into eternity."

He laid the scroll upon the lectern, its blank surface gleaming faintly, and placed the quill beside it.

"Take these. Write with your hand what your heart dares confess. Let it be false, and your name will vanish. Let it be true, and your tale will be sung among the constellations forever."

The chamber hushed, the shelves leaning as though straining to hear. The Sphinx stirred, her golden eyes igniting, and the Raven's wings twitched in anticipation.

Thoth's long hand rose, the quill still glowing faintly between his fingers. He gestured toward the dais of red stone, and the Sphinx stirred, her vast body shifting with a sound like grinding mountains.

"Behold," Thoth said, his voice low as the turning of ages, "the Guardian of Riddles. She is older than kings, older than empires, older even than the first song of men. None pass beyond her without answering what she asks. For her riddles are not games, but mirrors. They do not seek cleverness, but truth. She is the keeper of the unanswerable— yet answer her, and the path is opened."

The Sphinx rose to her full height, wings folded against her flanks, golden eyes fixed upon Snow with a gaze that was both terrible and beautiful. Her mane blazed like molten bronze in the glow of the ruby crystal, each strand a thread of fire. Snow felt small beneath her, as though she stood before a mountain wrought into living flesh, or before an idol given breath.

She drew closer, every step echoing on the starlit floor. The Raven shifted on its perch, feathers gleaming like midnight fire, but Snow's eyes were fixed on the Sphinx.

The creature's paws rested upon the stone as though upon the foundations of the world itself. Her wings curved above her like an archway, a threshold of judgment. The lines of her body—lion's strength, eagle's wings, woman's face—seemed to hold the essence of every trial Snow had endured: power, flight, and the reflection of her own humanity.

Snow's breath caught. This was no mere beast of riddles. She understood now why Thoth had called her the mirror. The Sphinx embodied the very question of existence: strength tempered by wisdom, beauty shadowed by ferocity, mortality bound to eternity.

The Tower waited in silence, as though creation itself leaned in for the riddle.

The Sphinx lowered her head, and when she spoke the Tower itself seemed to vibrate. Her voice was velvet thunder, a sound that reached not only Snow's ears but her very bones.

"I am the question that births your trials, the fire that tempers your soul. I am the thread that binds grief and grace. Without me, your story is not written. What am I?"

The words hung in the air, heavier than stone, brighter than flame.

Snow froze where she stood. The riddle echoed in her mind, repeating again and again, as though her own thoughts had become its chamber. She turned it over, tasting each word as if it were wine and ash on her tongue. *The question that births your trials… the fire that tempers your soul… the thread that binds grief and grace…*

144

Her heart quickened. Wonder filled her chest, not the wonder of enchantment, but the wonder of recognition—like a memory too vast to belong to one life alone. She knew the riddle was not asked to trick her, nor to test her wit, but to pierce her to the core and rattling the marrow of her bones, to make her reckon with what she had become.

Snow glanced at the lectern where the quill gleamed faintly, waiting. All she had to do was bend and write her answer. Yet still she lingered, her mind circling the riddle, again and again, as if some hidden key would reveal itself in the rhythm of its words.

The Tower listened in silence, the shelves leaning forward like a choir holding its breath.

The riddle pulsed in her veins. *The question that births your trials… the fire that tempers your soul… the thread that binds grief and grace…*

Her mind drifted, unbidden, through the shadowed gallery of all she had endured.

She saw again the crown of temptation gleaming alone upon the throne, the raven's eye burning as Set whispered of power. She felt the serpopard's coils, dragging her into the river—not as a beast to drown her, but as the wild, thrashing half of her own soul. She had faced it, embraced it, and in the silver glow of Khonshu, that part of her was returned: her emotions no longer an enemy, but her strength. She remembered the enchanted forest, where the breath of trees filled her veins with the truth that all lives are bound together. She felt the flames of sacrifice, when she laid down her soul for Dopey, faith holding her steady as chaos clawed at her. She saw the Chamber of the Scales, her heart trembling in Doc's hands, the terror of unworthiness meeting Anubis's solemn gaze. And lastly, the mirror shattering, Maat revealed at last in her quiet majesty, Snow's own voice confessing: *I was loved.*

The images flickered like starlight across the Tower's walls, so swift and quiet she wondered if she alone had seen them. They left her trembling, not from fear, but from awe—her pilgrimage unfolding not as a path of failure and suffering, but as a single tapestry woven through every trial.

Her lips parted, whispering the riddle to herself once more, tasting its weight. *Without me, your story is not written.*

Snow's eyes lowered to the waiting scroll.

The Tower held its breath. Even the constellations above seemed to still, waiting. Snow lingered before the scroll, her hand hovering, her thoughts circling the riddle like a bird caught in its own orbit.

Then—

A sudden, thunderous sneeze shattered the silence.

It tore through the chamber with comic violence, echoing up the spiral of shelves until it was as though the whole of creation had sneezed at once. Scrolls trembled. Dust leapt from forgotten ledges. A cloud of it swirled down in a glittering haze, catching the starlight as though the air itself were filled with falling constellations.

Snow gasped and turned. Sneezy stood behind her, red-eyed and sniffling, mortified and small in this place of grandeur. Yet his sneeze had done what reverence could not—it had broken the stillness. In the swirl of disturbed dust, something revealed itself upon the floor: a glowing shape in the constellation's shifting lines.

First, the apple, shining red as sin.

Snow's breath hitched. She had seen this shape before—it was where her pilgrimage began. And yet the pattern did not remain. The dust and starlight shifted again, threads weaving until the crest of her family burned before her in silver and flame. The room trembled as if her bloodline, her mortal flesh, were being claimed into the eternal record.

Then, slowly, the crest dissolved into something greater: the infinite geometry of the Flower of Life, its petals spinning outward in perfect symmetry, filling the chamber with a holy glow.

Snow's heart raced. She turned back to the scroll. The riddle pulsed in her chest. The constellations had spoken—yet still, only she could write the answer.

Snow's lips curved into the faintest smile. For the first time in what felt like lifetimes, it was not a mask, not a trembling of pretense, but a smile born from knowing. Tears slid quietly down her cheeks, warm and unashamed, shimmering in the light of the constellations. She no longer trembled. She knew.

Her hand reached forward, steady now. She lifted the quill. Its feather was heavier than it seemed, as though all of heaven leaned upon its weight. The scroll gleamed, waiting.

Snow lowered the quill to the page and began to write.

What she inscribed cannot be shown here, for her answer was her own.

***

And now—dear reader—it must be yours.

The Sphinx does not ask her riddle only of Snow White, nor does Thoth wait only for her confession. The Tower of Records watches all who walk, all who weep, all who hope. One day, you too will climb these stairs. You too will be handed the quill. And you too will be asked: **What am I?**

Do not look for the answer here, upon these pages. It will not be given to you. For only you can write it. Only you can weigh your own heart. Only you can face the truth at the end of your pilgrimage.

***

Snow's hand moved, the ink burning like fire and starlight across the scroll. The chamber shook as constellations aligned, as the Flower of Life blossomed in radiant perfection beneath her feet.

The last curve of her quill burned itself into the parchment. For a heartbeat, all was still.

Then the scroll shuddered. With a sudden roll, it snapped closed and rose into the air, glowing like a captured star. The quill followed, lifted as if by an unseen wind, its tip scattering sparks of molten light. Both spun upward in a spiral of radiance until they came to rest in the long, outstretched hands of Thoth.

The ibis-headed god received them with silent gravity, as though another volume had been added to the eternal shelves of creation. His dark eyes gleamed, but he spoke no word.

The Sphinx threw back her head. From her throat poured a roar so vast it seemed to shake the constellations loose from their moorings. The Tower itself trembled, scrolls quivering, stars rippling in response to her thunder.

And then—

The Raven moved.

With a single beat of its wings, the ruby crystal beneath it cracked, spilling crimson light across the floor. It beat them again, and the chamber filled with wind and storm, feathers whipping like black fire through the air. Scrolls rattled, shelves groaned, and the very constellations began to whirl in a furious dance.

Snow lifted her face to the gale, hair streaming, tears torn from her cheeks and scattered into the storm.

The flurry of wings grew deafening, filling every corner of the Tower with shadow and light.

<u>Epilogue</u>

Snow was swept into the in-between — not void, not silence, but a realm brimming with presence. Around her stood all who had walked beside her through the Pilgrimage: the gods of Egypt with their radiant forms, the guardians of chaos and light, the strange creatures that had tested her, Christian with his staff, and the raven circling ever above. And yet, no dwarfs. Not here.

The raven dipped lower, its wings scattering sparks of starlight, until all the deities and figures began to spiral with it, moving together as though bound in one eternal rhythm. The circle tightened, the shimmer deepened, and when the raven came so close its shadow brushed her cheek, it descended — folding into itself — and transformed with grace into Christian.

Snow laughed, tears streaming as wonder broke open within her. For now she saw the truth: every guide and trial, every voice that comforted or condemned, every hand that steadied or struck — all had been Him. He had told her she would not be alone, and He had kept his word.

Christian's gaze met hers, ancient and tender all at once. His voice was steady as eternity.

"Welcome home, my child. We have eagerly waited for your arrival."

Before her shimmered the Celestial Gates, vast and golden. At their center glowed a keyhole, pulsing with light. The ankh upon her neck burned with fire, and she lifted it free. In her palm it turned, transfigured, into a ruby-red key — its handle shaped like the apple that had once doomed her.

Snow placed it in the lock. The gates opened, and though their passage was silent, from within there rose a sound — voices cheering, laughing, rejoicing. The dwarfs. Their joy thundered like a welcome long prepared.

Snow turned, and her face shone with peace beyond sorrow, joy beyond grief. Her lips trembled into a smile as she whispered in her mother's tongue:

"Mama... Papa... endlich."

Christian did not follow her through the gates. Instead, he turned, as though his eyes pierced the veil beyond time itself. And when he spoke, it was no longer to Snow — it was at His favorite witness to this very pilgrimage… you.

"And so it will be with you. You will walk your own Pilgrimage, and you will face your own trials. But you will never be alone. For I will be with you, in shadow and in light, in sorrow and in joy. And when your journey is complete, I will welcome you home. All of my children — with open arms."

Welcome to the

Legends Reborn Chronicles

The Legends Reborn Chronicles is our grand saga that reimagines classic myths and fairy tales from around the world. From Norse legends to Greek myths and the mysteries of the Amazon, each book opens a portal to a world where old tales find new life. Expect epic adventures, intricate characters, and a tapestry of stories that connect the past to a new, magical future.

This is where legends are reborn.

Blue Box 29

Mark and Jane are the creative and life partners behind the stories you love. As co-authors, they weave together their shared passion for mythology, fairy tales, and a touch of real-life adventure. They're not just partners in creativity, but also in life, faith, and the journey of making the world a little more magical—one tale at a time.

Inside our World:

Step beyond the veil and into the heart of Blue Box 29 — where myth, memory, and meaning intertwine. This is more than a brand; it's a sanctuary for storytellers, seekers, and soul-builders. Inside our world, every page we write, every image we create, and every service we offer is rooted in transformation — born from the belief that healing, creativity, and purpose are not separate paths, but one luminous journey. Whether you're drawn to the sacred, the strange, or the beautifully in-between, you'll find a home here. Welcome to the myth beneath the mirror.

Our Vision:

We envision a world where stories don't just entertain — they awaken. At Blue Box 29, our vision is to restore the sacred bond between creativity and the soul, to craft works that echo through the heart long after the final page is turned. We believe in brave art, in myth reborn, and in the power of personal truth to spark collective transformation. Whether through books, wellness services, or curated spiritual tools, we aim to light the way for others to rediscover who they are — not by escaping reality, but by revealing the magic within it.

www.ingramcontent.com/pod-product-compliance
Lightning Source LLC
Chambersburg PA
CBHW020022030726
47499CB00007B/2230